THE DEVIL'S TRIANGLE

TONI DE PALMA

The Devil's Triangle
Toni De Palma

www.ellysianpress.com

The Devil's Triangle
© Copyright Toni De Palma 2016. All rights reserved.

Print ISBN: 978-1-941637-25-8
Second Edition

Editor: Jen Ryan, Imagine That Editing
Cover Art: M Joseph Murphy

DEDICATION

To the one who brings out my devilish side.
You know who you are.

"The Devil inside, the Devil inside, every single one of us the Devil inside." – INXS

CHAPTER 1

△

Saint Pete peered over the rim of his glasses. "I don't know, Lucinda. The records show that this boy's life has been one appalling incident after another." He held up the paper he'd been reading so that the rest of us could see. Except for a big black X, the paper was blank.

Yup, that pretty much summed me up. I'd been in limbo for what seemed like forever. It was like a reality show competition to see if all of the trouble I'd stirred up down on Earth would send me into the fiery depths for all eternity.

"Oh, I hardly think your paper gives an honest opinion of him." Lucy flipped her shiny black hair over her shoulder and giggled. This was no little-girl giggle. The sound that slipped from her mouth felt a little dangerous, like quicksand. She'd earned her spot at the table when she'd split from her brother, Lucifer, crossing party lines. A lot of guys would have been put off by a chick whose brother was the Devil. Not me. In my eyes, it made Lucy that much hotter.

Saint Pete frowned. "What's on your mind, Lucinda?"

"Well, compared to some of the people from my old neighborhood, I don't think Cooper's half bad. In fact, I find him quite redeemable." Lucy winked at me. Was she flirting?

Whether this was a game to Lucy or she honestly believed I belonged in Heaven, I didn't really care. In life, I'd been a fly-by-the-seat-of-your-pants kind of guy. Life was just a series of moments – bad ones, mostly. What happened once all those moments got used up had never been a question high on my priority list. But there I was, standing front and center at my very own Judgment Day.

The old guy next to Lucy woke up long enough to join the conversation. Every once in a while, the three of them would look back at me as if they were measuring my fitness for Heaven. Pure stupidity. Didn't my record prove I'd never fit in anywhere?

All the hush-hush eventually broke down, and when he turned around to face me, Saint Pete's face looked pink.

"This is insane, Lucinda!" he said.

"I think it's a great idea!" Like a hunter looking through her scope, Lucy trained her eyes on me.

Saint Pete sucked in a breath.

"What's a great idea?" I asked. None of them answered my question.

I looked at the old guy. He was just opening his mouth, giving the impression that he had something to say. But all of sudden his head drooped and he started to snore.

Oblivious to his partner, Saint Pete continued to argue with Lucy. "You honestly want to send him back? Doesn't humankind have enough waste already? If we send him back, we'll only be adding to the landfill."

Ouch! Okay, so my record back home was less than stellar, but did he really have to resort to name calling?

Lucy cooed hypnotically, "But Petey. We all make mistakes, don't we? And you do know how *He* feels about things like this."

He, that He? Talk about name dropping. Even I had to admit that having a direct line to the Big Guy was kind of pimp.

Saint Peter squirmed in his chair as if he was actually considering Lucy's suggestion. "You do have a point. It does bother *Him* tremendously when someone squanders their potential."

Ick. If there was one word I hated it was potential. Over the years, I'd heard it so many times that whenever someone said it I was overcome with the urge to strip down naked and slide down a rope. Really, really fast.

"You're not using your potential, Cooper."

"Don't you care about your potential, Cooper?"

"Not everyone has as much potential as you do, Cooper."

Yuck.

When I'd gotten here, I'd figured that, along with the school I'd burned down, I'd extinguished all the potential I had left. Apparently, it didn't work that way.

As I opened my mouth to say something, Lucy made a quick zipping motion across her lips and my own were sealed.

Crap.

As I tried to pry my lips open, Lucy campaigned even harder for her idea. Like a top-notch politician, she pulled out a flow chart. "Let's look at the facts. Your numbers have been declining lately. Do you really want to give Lucifer another win?" Lucy leaned in closer to show Saint Pete her charts. When she did, she managed, not so accidently, to brush her hand against his wrist.

Talk about heat.

Saint Pete cleared his throat. "Um . . . Yes. I see what you mean, Lucinda."

Hey! Whose Judgment Day was this anyway? I should have an opinion on the matter, too. Since my mouth was no good, I shook my head and waved my hands. Instead of letting me speak, Lucy blew me a kiss.

Lucy stoked Saint Pete's fire some more. "If you're

3

concerned that I don't have Cooper's well-being in mind, then just look at me. Haven't I turned out well?" Lucy leaned forward some more. Talk about giving Saint Pete a peek at her global assets.

I could tell Saint Pete was struggling. Who wouldn't be? And I'd bet twenty more lifetimes that what Saint Pete was thinking had nothing to do with me.

"Very well! We'll give him a second chance," Saint Pete said. Under his breath, he added, "May God help us."

Above my head, I heard a rumble that seemed to go unnoticed by everyone else in the room.

The invisible stitches that had been holding my lips together suddenly ripped open. "You're really doing it? You're sending me back to my old life?" I sputtered.

"Your old life?" The moment Lucy's laugh rang out of her mouth, I, too, realized the impossibility.

"That wouldn't be entirely possible now, would it?" Saint Pete said. "Not with the obituary all written out and the tombstone in place. That would be a logistical nightmare. Just think of the paperwork!"

He was right. I had no place to go back to. Not only would it be confusing for everyone, including me, but I seriously doubted the people back in Florida would be waiting for me with *Welcome Home* banners.

There went Lucy again, looking me up, down and sideways. I couldn't help it. Those emerald green eyes made me spazzy, producing a tectonic shift in my pants.

"I know the perfect place for you!" she told me. "There's a high school in New Jersey. And a girl. Her name is Grace. I want you to find her."

Grace? As in Amazing Grace and that whole saving a poor wretch like me thing? While Lucy had a lot going for her in the bootie bombshell department, she sure did lack subtlety.

Before I could ask what it was I was supposed to do

once I found Grace, Saint Pete launched into a lecture on the rules. "Keep in mind, Cooper, this is a second chance. Not a free ride. You will have just one month to go back down to Earth and redeem yourself. Once you have, we will summon you back here, and we will judge whether you go up or down." With this, Saint Pete made a motion with his thumb downward.

If I didn't go, there was no doubt about it. I was going directly to Hell.

But what if I did take Lucy up on her offer and I found Grace? If she was cute and I could convince her to take a ride on my stone pony, maybe the two of us could create a whole other kind of amazing. There was something else, too. What that something was I couldn't say or even make out too clear in my mind. Whatever it was felt like a flutter deep in my chest.

"Okay," I said.

With the way Lucy shrugged, I doubted I really ever had a choice in the matter. Lucy pointed to a spot with her long, red nails. "Stand there."

Crap. I was in the suds.

Somebody must have turned up the wattage because the fluttery feeling in my chest got stronger. In fact it was freaking me out a little. Not one for nerves, I secretly hoped that wherever I was headed they had some deodorant waiting for me.

Lucy's voice rang in my ear. "Take a breath, Cooper."

Rather than just one, I took a whole handful of them. The light started feeling good, warm, like melted marshmallow topping. Until I realized that I was the nut fudge sundae.

"Bon voyage!" Lucy trilled.

The flutter in my chest became more like a battering ram, hitting me hard in the solar plexus. I was dead, and it still felt as if the life was being sucked out of me.

I held it together long enough to give Lucy a little wink. Then I took another breath, and I settled into the feeling. "Beam me up, Scotty."

And just like that I was toast.

CHAPTER 2

△

Someone swatted me on the back of my head. When I looked up, twenty-five pairs of eyes were staring at me.

"Ahem," the man at the front of the room coughed out. He was holding a leather-bound book in his hand and wore silver-framed glasses. Standing at the tall stump of wood podium like he was, I thought I was back in church. But then I saw the kid in the desk in front of me, and I knew this was no funeral. Or was it?

"Please refrain from drooling on the furniture, Mr. Wanderman. The taxpayers wouldn't approve," Mr. Preacher-teacher man said to me.

Some big kid, two rows over, who looked like he'd been crammed into his desk, snickered. "Good one, Mr. Reynolds," he said.

Mr. Reynolds looked bored. He could barely manage a smirk for the kid when he said, "Yes, well, I'll let my agent know you approve of the entertainment, Mr. Richards." Then he proceeded to slide his finger over the top of his desk. When he saw the dust, he added, "Perhaps, based on your endorsement, my agent can negotiate a better room for me."

I couldn't believe it! Lucy had actually gone and done it. I was alive. Again.

Looking around the room, I wasn't really sure that it

was the perfect place that Lucy said it would be. I mean it wasn't like the pre-convict program I'd been going to before my little arson incident, but this place was no prep school either. On the other hand, it kind of looked familiar.

Without thinking how it might come off, I leaned forward and said to the bacne kid, "Hey, this isn't the place where they filmed *High School Musical*, is it?"

As if *I* was the leper, the kid inched forward and didn't answer.

As Mr. Reynolds wrote on the board, my eyes skipped over everyone else that was there. With the exception of the dumb beef ball and some punk chick by the window, the rest of them looked like their mothers still brushed their teeth.

The kid to my right had a backpack that wasn't zipped. As I wondered whether or not the backpack contained anything worth stealing, Mr. Reynolds flapped his gums about some guy named Tom.

"Mr. Wanderman," Mr. Reynolds asked as he wrote on the board, "What is your opinion about King Lear's conclusion that the old beggar, Tom, was actually a prophet?"

My eyes were still on the backpack. If the kid didn't have a cell phone or an iPod, I'd have settled for some lunch. Getting recycled sure made a person hungry.

"Mr. Wanderman?"

Whoever this Wanderman kid was, he was about as dick-brained as me when it came to this literature crap because he still wasn't answering.

The girl who sat behind me poked me with her pencil. "Answer him, stupid," she said to me.

Then I got it. *I* was Mr. Wanderman.

Ha! Ha! Nice touch, Lucy. But instead of just thinking this, I made the mistake of actually saying it. Twenty-five pairs of eyes looked at me again like I'd just come from some alien planet. I guess they weren't so far off the mark.

This time Mr. Reynolds mustered up an expression that was somewhat close to sympathetic. "Oh, please don't tell me football has rotted your brain, Mr. Wanderman."

Football, too? Lucy had to be kidding.

Mr. Reynolds tapped his chalk on the board where he'd written the words, *King Lear? Hapless or Hopeless?*

I looked at the words and didn't like how they seemed to be talking about me.

While the setting was new, I was still the same old same old. "Uh, sorry, Mr. Reynolds. I've got nothing for you on that one," I said.

Back at Arsonville Tech, this sort of attitude was perfectly acceptable to the teachers. Heck. Attitude was half of what helped you to survive. The rest of your survival depended on how fast you could run. But Mr. Reynolds didn't react the way most teachers did to my mouth.

As if he could never fill his lungs up with quite enough air, he sighed. Then he moved to his desk where he jotted down something in his grade book.

Bacne Boy turned around and glared. "Busted!"

The rest of them looked at me like I was nothing more than a big dish of bad sushi. Okay, so the rules around here were a bit more traditional, but what did I care? Did these Grade A eggheads honestly think a red check next to my name made a difference in the long run and that your permanent record really could catch up to you?

Okay, so much for that theory. Still, in my past life kids like Bacne Boy would have carried rolls of toilet paper around with them on account of me. It wasn't that I was a big guy or even particularly strong. What made me someone to avoid was the fact that I would do anything on account of I'd always felt that I'd had nothing to lose. And guys with nothing to lose were always the most dangerous ones, especially to themselves.

When he was done, Mr. Reynolds looked up at us. "I'd

like to remind all of you that, if you don't pass Junior Honors English, you will be forced to go to summer school. And since this building has no air conditioning, all I can say is that summer school can be quite hellish."

"Hellish, right!" I blurted out.

Mr. Reynolds' hand hovered over his pen, ready to check me off again. "Is there a problem, Mr. Wanderman?"

Since I'd just touched down on this planet again, I figured it was probably a good idea to fly under the radar. At least for now.

Biting my tongue, I said, "Um . . . No problem."

"So we're on board?" he asked everybody, but mainly he was talking to me. His silver glasses glinted. A chill ran across my shoulders in the otherwise airless room.

Like a freakin' puppet, I nodded.

Mr. Reynolds went back to writing on the board. With the attention off of me, I figured I'd better get down to business before my mouth popped open and I said something that would land me in detention for the next month. Scanning the room for this Grace chick, my eyes landed on a long-haired beauty two seats in from the door. The girl had cleavage that would make any red blooded teenage boy hail the first cab to Hell if he could have just one crack at her.

Please, please, please, let her be Grace!

Mr. Reynolds started spouting off about King Lear again. "Perhaps King Lear was on to something," he said. "Perhaps, unlike the rest of the people, King Lear had a moment of clarity. When faced with Old Tom, maybe, unlike the rest of you, he was able to see what was hidden beneath the beggar's clothes."

As he droned on and on, my eyes took an accounting of each girl in the class. Another cute blonde sat two aisles over. Another excellent Grace candidate. But the girl's name turned out to be Ayslan instead.

Good thing she wasn't Grace. When Ayslan opened her

mouth, she was like a geyser. Big words exploded out of her. The only thing cuddling up with her at night was the dictionary.

Reynolds closed his leather book, a puff of dust wafting out from the thin, yellow pages. Did people pay money for old books like that?

"Let's shift gears a little bit," Mr. Reynolds said. "Everyone pair up with a partner."

That sounded good to me. I got up and headed over to Miss Rocky Mountains, but another guy nearly neutered himself on his desk as he lunged ahead of me.

My eyes darted around the room. Everyone, except for the one punk rock girl, was already paired up. I knew it. Just because I'd gotten a second chance didn't mean my luck would be any better.

I wove in and out of people, making my way over to the other side of the room. Even though she wasn't looking at me as I approached, the first thing I noticed about the girl was her steely intensity as she dug the point of her lead pencil into an already well-mutilated desk top.

I must have been hovering there for longer than I thought because Mr. Reynolds came up from behind me and said, "Shall I print you a formal invitation?"

Little Miss Pink Parasite looked up and threw me a wary glance. Then she went back to the process of exfoliating her desk. Talk about flakes. As bad as I'd been, I'd always made it my business to steer away from nutcases like that.

I stared at the empty chair next to the girl and wondered how many milliseconds it had taken the last guy to vacate.

With no other choice, I pointed to the empty seat and said about the dweebiest thing anyone could ever say. "Is this seat taken?"

Okay so I wasn't exactly Pitbull. In my head I was, but the smooth maneuvers I saw myself making in my imagination never came out right in real life.

"Well, unless your invisible friend just took a crap on that seat, yeah, I guess it's okay for you to sit there," she said back.

Great! Part of the reason I'd always stayed away from chicks like this was because they had the uncanny ability to sniff out the fact that I was totally inexperienced.

I guess it was good to know that, in my brief absence, the world and the people in it were just as crappy as they always were. Feeling like a neutered gerbil, I slumped down in the desk across from the girl.

Mr. Reynolds explained the assignment. "Using just one notebook, I want you to take turns having a silent conversation. Pass the paper back and forth. One person will ask a question, the other one will respond and so on and so forth. And remember! Just like King Lear, it's important to reveal yourself."

This last detail got a lot of snickers.

"Maturity, people!" Mr. Reynolds shook his head. Then he went back to his podium where he opened his leather book and started to read to himself.

"What a whack job," I said to the girl, forgetting I was supposed to hate her. I also forgot that I was supposed to know certain stuff. "Is he always that weird?" I asked her.

"It's all about the tights," she said.

"The what?"

She rolled her eyes at me, but then she made like she was snapping the waistband of her pants. Then she pointed her chin at Mr. Reynolds.

"You're kidding, right?" I said.

She shook her head. "Nope. He wears them all the time. I think it helps him get in the mood."

Feeling like a total idiot, I couldn't help but sneak another peek. Was that bulge what I thought it was?

The girl shook her head and laughed. When she threw back her head, the tiny diamond stud in her nose sparkled.

She wasn't bad looking. In fact, she was kind of cute.

"What are you looking at?" she said. Her tone was strange, not as threatening as I was expecting, but just short of rolling out the welcome mat, too.

She must have caught herself, because she tucked away her smile and said, "This is supposed to be a silent conversation."

Everyone was already huddled up, scrawling stuff down in their notebooks. Everyone looked way ahead of us. Kiss asses.

I hadn't thought to look under my desk for a notebook. With none of my own, the girl pulled out her notebook. Instead of using the whole thing, she tore out a half sheet of paper. If this was up to her, this was obviously going to be short and sweet.

My first impulse was to ask the girl her name, but I'd already done plenty to blow my cover.

The nameless girl went first. As she stared at the paper, thinking about what to write, I finished checking her out. When she wasn't busy stripping the varnish off of the furniture, her face softened up. Though the spiky, pink hair really didn't do anything for her, the diamond stud in her nose was a nice touch. Five gold loops ran up her left ear lobe, reminding me of the trapeze rings on the playground. Her right ear had a tiny hole in it, too, but the hole was empty, just a small indentation against the soft, pink flesh that was otherwise unmarred. I started fantasizing about all the other soft parts of her.

She scribbled something down fast and slipped the half sheet of paper back over to me. Looking down at what she'd written, a warm flush of heat spread up from my neck.

No, I didn't wake up late and forget to put in my other earring.

I looked up and for the briefest second our eyes locked on each other. "How?" I said.

13

"This is a silent conversation," Mr. Reynolds interjected before I could finish.

Our desks were face to face and there it was again, that little sparkle. That time it wasn't the diamond in her nose, but the sparkle in her eye that set off the flutter in my chest all over again.

Quickly, I scribbled back. *How did you know what I was thinking?* I slid the piece of paper back across my desk.

As she wrote her answer down, I couldn't help but notice the inch of skin that winked out at me from under her sleeve. The beginnings of a tattoo teased me. I imagined that tattoo trailing up her white skin. Like a hungry bird following a line of crumbs, I wanted to follow that trail.

The piece of paper came back to me.

It's easy to tell what's on a guy's mind, because they're usually just thinking about one thing.

Snagged!

The girl pointed her pencil at me, her face revealing more than a little bit of expectation. Underneath the heavy eyeliner was a fake birth mark, coyly placed on her right cheek. Like an old Mustang convertible, she had more to her than just a bad paint job.

I could have just asked her name, but I decided to ask her something else instead.

I scribbled, *Do you believe in second chances?*

When I slid the paper back over to her, I was not ready for her reaction. She winced, the look on her face as painful as ice cream soaking into a root canal. But just as fast as the pained look had come, it receded. Her face contorted into a pissed look that I was more than familiar with from all the pissed looks I'd collected over the years. What was the big deal?

"Wrap it up, people," Reynolds announced.

The protective bubble that the two of us had existed in briefly now popped, leaving only a sticky residue of dissatisfaction behind. Whatever it was I'd been feeling flitted away. Now when I looked up, the pretty little sparkle was gone, replaced instead by two nuclear warheads aimed directly at me. What was this girl's problem?

So much for baring my soul and being honest and all that other crap. There was still a little more time before the bell rang. As the other students grabbed their books, Mr. Reynolds kept reading. I tried to keep my eyes on anything but her.

The bell rang and everyone who had something better to do went to go do it. That left me.

I looked down at my desk and was surprised to find the answer to my question after all.

Kiss off!

Nice. Real nice.

As I got up, I was about to ball the paper up and toss it in the garbage can. That's when I saw the name. Grace Sanders.

Not believing my bad luck, I shook my head. Then I realized luck had nothing to do with this. The little fiasco had Lucy's name written all over it.

"Very funny, Lucy," I said as loud as I could. That time you can bet I wanted to be heard.

CHAPTER 3

△

In the hall, kids slammed their lockers and started heading for the buses. As I was trying to figure out what to do next, someone grabbed me from behind.

"Let . . . go of me, you freak," I sputtered. From the size of the tree trunk lodged under my neck I could tell that the guy had a good forty or fifty pounds on me. Before saying okay to Lucy, I should have negotiated a bigger build, a thicker neck, and maybe some six-pack abs while I was at it. Too late now. The guy had such a tight grip on me that every time I wriggled, the hair on his arm chaffed my face like a cheap roll of toilet paper.

I did still have some tricks up my sleeve. Shifting my weight back, I brought my foot up and wham! The douchebag's toes went crunch.

The tree trunk yelped and loosened his grip long enough for me to wiggle away.

Spinning around, I was ready for whatever came next. The muscles in my legs were coiled and ready to spring. Instead of pulling a move, the big ape just looked at me like I was the one with the problem. It wasn't only him, either. A few kids stood at the end of the hall, gawking. Obviously, their lily-white existences had never exposed them to someone like me. One of them disappeared around the corner, probably to go get a grown-up who could solve this problem for them. Yeah, right. Not even the shrinks, who got paid the big bucks, had ever been able to figure me out.

"Whoa, Coopman. Chill out, will ya?"

Coopman? Did I know this guy?

In the end, it wasn't fear, but the way the guy peeled back his lips in a big-ass grin that made me relax.

"Come on, Coop. Coach is gonna be pissed if we're late for practice," he said. "And I hate to tell you, man, but that jock strap excuse of yours is getting old."

The pug-nosed ape was faster than I thought because before I knew it, he leaned in close. At first I thought he was going to take another swipe at me. Instead, he fisted up his paw and ruffled my hair. Then he laughed some more like I was the best entertainment he'd had all day.

Something Mr. Reynolds had said in class suddenly hit me. Crap! Not only did I know this guy, but we were freakin' teammates! And by the way he kept calling me Coopman, maybe even friends.

The kid who'd run off had never come back, but the ones still standing around watching us had something in their eyes. Respect. Being a jock was hardly how I'd earned respect in the past. But for now, I'd take it.

The guy started walking and, though it was against my better judgment, I followed. Seriously, Lucy's potshots were endless. What else did she have written on her Things That Will Royally Piss Cooper Off list?

As we walked, a cute redhead sashayed by and said, "Hi, Blake."

So the Yeti had a name. I was starting to think that my atoms had gotten seriously rearranged during the trip, because I honestly wished that this guy might be kind of cool. If nothing else, he might be able to introduce me to some cute girls.

We ended up in the locker room. The place was already

filled with guys. If Lucy had wanted me to find a new crew to hang with, couldn't she have picked a better smelling bunch? The guys reeked with a combination of You the Man deodorant, jock cheese, and a mega dose of I Want My Mommy desperation.

Blake walked up to a kid who was sitting on a bench, spraying his sneakers.

"Got the crud again, Jimbo?" Blake picked up a towel and snapped it at the kid's head.

Jimbo twisted up his mouth and frowned. Even though he was bigger than Blake by a good couple of inches, for some reason he held back. I looked at the kid, wondering why he would take Blake's crap when it was obvious he could stuff him in a locker without breaking a sweat.

As I was wondering about the guy, I realized something. "Hey! You're the kid in my English class," I said to him.

The two of them looked at me like I had a palm tree growing out of my nose. A second later, the look of confusion on Blake's face morphed into a grin. "Ha! Good one, Coopman. It's not like you haven't known Jimmy since kindergarten!"

"Yeah, those were good times," Jimmy said, a wistful expression on his face. "Remember how you and me stopped up the toilet with wads of toilet paper?" he said.

I went along with it and said, "Oh, yeah!"

"Freaked Trischa Davies out. She started crying. Waa! Waa! About those dumb shoes of hers." Jimmy laughed.

"Oh, yeah! Remember what a princess she was?" I said.

"You oughta know," Blake said. "You brought her to prom last year."

"Uh, right," I said. This was weird terrain, but of course I had to push it. "Remember that other little kid? The one who started crying because he said he couldn't swim?" I windmilled my arms over my head like I was doing the back stroke.

18

Lucky for me, the muscle in Jimmy's body left no room for brain cells. "Yeah! I remember that." Jimmy laughed again.

And so did I, but not for the same reason.

"I don't remember that," Blake said. He cocked his head to one side, looking at me like it was the first time he was seeing me.

"Um . . . Yeah," I said. Done with my back stroking, I stuck my hands in my pockets where they couldn't get me into any more trouble.

Surprisingly, it was Jimmy this time who threw me a lifeline. "Aw, Blake. How could you remember anything about kindergarten? You spent the whole year in the time-out chair."

Blake snarled at Jimmy. I couldn't resist getting the last word in. "Yeah, it's a miracle you don't have a permanent splinter up your ass from all that sitting," I said.

Some of the other guys started laughing at Blake, whose granite features flushed red. I didn't care. I might have just made myself an enemy, but it felt good to be me again.

Blake turned his back on me. He opened up his locker and started getting changed for practice. Staring at the rows of lockers in front of me, I suddenly realized that I now had a different problem on my hands.

Blake must have noticed my hesitation because there was that same look again. It was the look of a crowd of people at the zoo, only I was the genetically mutated ostrich.

Instead of calling me on it, Blake said, "Didn't I tell you? The janitor fixed your locker." With that, he made a fist and popped the locker next to him right open.

"Oh, yeah. Great," I said.

With that, Blake went back to taping himself up like a mummy. Maybe he wasn't such a bad guy after all.

Sneaking glances, I watched how the other guys suited up. Other than feeling like a complete dork, I managed to put on my shoulder pads and knee guards without too much of a problem. As I laced up my chest protector, I watched as one guy snapped his jock strap in another guy's face. Even with the new trappings, I could tell I was the same old me. If one of those guys tried that on me, they'd be sorry.

As I put on the pair of cleats I'd found in my locker, the day of the fire wormed itself back into my conscious mind. No matter how tightly I laced my shoes, I couldn't squeeze the image out of my head. I'd been going to the store that day when some guy with dreads started talking smack to me. He was acting all rasta-gangsta with his tie-dyed T-shirt and frayed jeans. The weird thing was that the dude was paper white. I'd never seen an albino Rastafarian before, so I couldn't help but stare.

"Hey, pansy!" The Rastafarian dude called out to me. "What're you lookin' at? Don't you know the only place pansies like you belong are in an old lady's yard?"

I should have just kept walking, especially because his bad ass ways looked downright stupid on his lily-white ass. I should have kept my mind on the Snickers I was planning to buy at the store, but what with the whoo-hooing from the other guys in the albino's crew, I just couldn't ignore it.

I started shoveling shit right back.

"I may be a pansy, but that old lady you're talking about? She's your grandmother and I've got my roots all up in her!" I yelled back.

Who knew an albino could turn so many shades of red. He wasn't the only thing that got red. My ass was red and blue and purple. Afterwards, I took that anger and ran with it, straight to the school.

Looking down at my fists now, I opened and closed my hands. To someone else, it might look as if I was getting ready to haul off and punch someone. At the very least, it might have seemed like I had a weird tic. But what I saw were the invisible scars the Tickler crew had expertly buffed away.

"Earth to Coop!" Blake rapped his fist on my head. Lucky for me, he was holding back. Those big ham hocks of his could have fed a family of twenty on Thanksgiving. "Are you gonna get your ass in gear or what?" Blake asked. Apparently, he was over the whole splinter comment.

I looked around. Most of the guys were already gone. I closed up my locker, reminding myself that my memories were history. It was time to have some fun.

On our way out, some guy poked his head into the locker room. "Hey, Blake. Your girlfriend's outside. She says she skipped lunch and she wants your wiener." The guy cracked up at his own joke.

At first I thought Blake might get pissed. Instead he smirked and said, "Aw! Let her wait."

The guy shrugged like it really didn't matter to him either way.

I jogged onto the field behind Blake and some of the rest of the guys. Even with my helmet on, I could feel the sunlight warm on my face and arms. Not only did the sun feel good, but it made everything, the grass, the bleachers, even the goal posts, look brighter and more alive.

Well-run as it was, the afterlife had been a real bore. No one ever had a hair out of place, and people walked around all woo-woo like they'd just finished a yoga marathon. There weren't even any trash cans on account of there was never any trash. To me, it all felt flat.

I was hoping that Heaven had a little more action going for it. In the meantime, I knelt down and ran my hands over the blades of green grass. I'd never noticed before how mysterious dirt smelled, like there were layers and layers of history in that dirt and the worms that lived in it got to pass through that history on a daily basis. If Heaven didn't work out, I wondered if Lucy could turn me into a worm.

"Wanderman! Stop horsing around and get over here!"

I looked up. A short, stocky guy with very little neck was waving me over to where the rest of the dimwits had fallen into a circle around him.

When I merged with the rest of them, Blake came up to me. He was standing so close that he all but blocked out the sun, leaving me in shadow.

I threw him a look that translated into, Back off, will ya?

Clearly he wasn't getting the message. Instead he leaned in closer, the onions on his breath strong enough to topple the Eiffel Tower. "What's with you today, man?" he whispered.

Okay, so if Lucy wanted Blake and me to be buds, then why did I have such a strong repulsion for the guy?

Ignoring the question, I looked straight ahead. I told myself I wasn't here to make friends. I was here for me. No, nix that. I was here for Grace. Whatever that meant.

The guy with no neck turned out to be the coach. As he called roll, I soaked up as much sun as possible and pretended like I belonged.

CHAPTER 4

Coach called out names, checking them off from his clipboard as he went along. "Dwyer! Feinstein! Richards!"

I thought there was no way my name was going to be on that list. But wouldn't you know . . .

"Wanderman!"

Before I could control it, my hand shot up and I said, "Here!" My voice came out sounding puny, like it didn't even belong to me. Another side effect from my trip, no doubt. I shook my body, trying to work out the kinks. This gave Blake another reason to toss me one of his dirty looks.

Coach kept on with his list. After me came a guy named Ulrich and one named Zubeck. I did my best to blend in. When someone spit, I chugged a loogie. When someone else scratched his jock, I did a little dance and adjusted myself. The funny thing was no one seemed to notice or care. They all took it for granted that I belonged there. Everyone except Blake, that is. He was hovering so close I could see up into his nose and count the hairs.

Coach began a talk about strategy and team work. I ignored all the rah-rah stuff and tried to get my head straight. What was I doing there? Okay, so if I was going to be honest with myself, it came down to one thing. Being a virgin.

Dying wasn't so bad. But dying a virgin? That sucked

the big one.

But it wasn't just about the sex. No matter how great Heaven might be, I couldn't imagine that it could trump being with an amazing girl. As much as I liked to shovel my feelings under the rug, the butterflies that lived in my gut liked to come out every once in a while to give me a nudge. As much as I hated to admit it, I still had dreams and, like it or not, Blake might have been my best bet for an intro to the ladies.

Speaking of Blake, he'd moved away a bit. Over the crowd of muscle, I saw him off on the edge of the group, his attention focused on something that had nothing to do with football.

Across the field, to the left of where we stood, the home team bleachers sat all sparkly and new. The rickety, rusted seats on the other side of the field that were reserved for visitors were a sharp contrast. A couple of girls were sitting midway up the bleachers, their hands in their laps so the slight breeze wouldn't flap up their skirts. Blake was a dog, but I had to give him credit for his taste. These girls were hot.

But it wasn't the girls that had caught Blake's attention. He was staring at the hill where the school sat. Some crazy person was careening down the hill like a log being rolled. What an idiot!

"Crazy bitch," someone next to me said. It was Blake who spoke. While I'd been watching, he'd snuck back in next to me without me noticing.

The person popped up and shook themselves off. That was when I saw the hair.

I glanced back and forth between Blake and Grace, but then Coach yelled, "Get into position!"

The only position I was familiar with was the crouch-down-don't-let-the-cops-burn-your-ass position. I took a chance and stuck myself in the line. With my butt up high and my head down low, I wondered again why football was considered such a manly sport.

I knew I was doing it wrong. Not only didn't I feel like a man's man, but Coach was yelling my name again.

Popping my head up, Coach said, "Wanderman! What are you doing?"

Trying to keep myself out of Hell was what I should have said, but with the heavy uniform and the sweat pouring down my face, I wasn't sure there was much of a difference. If only Lucy had sent me down with some kind of manual, kind of like a playbook. But I was quickly getting the hint that Lucy had no intention of making this easy on me.

Blake stepped up for me. While I was pleased, I also hoped he didn't expect any payback.

"Aw! Coach," he said. "Coopman just wants to get back in the game."

What? No, this wasn't the kind of rescue I was hoping for.

"Well, he can get back in the game when the doctor says he can," Coach said to both of us. "For now, I'm not risking permanent injury to that ankle."

Ankle?

Blake patted me on the backside. "Sorry about that, Coopman," he said. If it wasn't for the way he looked at me, like he genuinely felt sorry for me, I would have hiked the ball straight to his groin.

I was no fool. When I saw a life boat passing, I didn't think twice about jumping right in. "Yeah, doctor's orders, I guess." Probably laying it on a little too thick, I limped out of formation.

Ankle. Good one. Score one for old Luce. Maybe she did have my back after all.

As I made my way off the field, I noticed Grace sitting on the bottom bleacher. Her head was down, and she was scribbling in her notebook. Remembering I had a job to do and only one month to do it, I lost the limp and headed her way.

Knowing Hell would get HBO a lot sooner than Grace would offer me an invite, I plopped down next to her. "Who're you telling to screw off now?" I asked.

The moment I did, Grace looked up at me. I could tell she was surprised I'd dared to invade her precious space. But not as surprised as I was. Being this close to her, the flutter was back. This time the butterflies felt supercharged. They snapped and popped and hummed, just like one of those electric boxes you find on the side of the road.

Though it made no sense to, I leaned away, scared Grace might hear.

"What?" Grace pulled her collar to her nose and took a whiff.

"No!" I said, realizing how she was taking it. "It's not you. You smell fine."

Grace looked at me like I was on something.

Eager to shift gears, I pointed to the notebook on her lap. "So is that like some kind of popularity list you're writing? You know, who's hot and who's not?" Was there anything in that notebook about me?

Grace rolled her eyes.

"I mean, that is what girls think about isn't it? I mean, who's prettier than who and who's going after some other girl's boyfriend?"

Grace's back stiffened. Though she didn't say anything, she glared at me intensely, as if she was casting a spell over me. She was probably wishing me into a rock. After all, I was sinking fast. The conversations I'd always had with girls had been mostly in my head. Those had come out a lot smoother. Maybe no matter what magic Lucy had up her sleeve, when it came to the opposite sex, I was destined to be lame.

"What?" Grace demanded.

"Um, nothing." Though I'd resisted the idea at first, I was happy I'd worn a cup.

"It's weird," she said. "It's like you were away, but today you're different."

That odd closeness I'd felt before returned, but I couldn't jeopardize blowing my cover. Being a big James Bond fan, I did my best 007 and leaned in seductively. "I didn't go anywhere, babe. I'm right here where I want to be. With you."

Grace frowned. Okay, I was no Sean Connery, but she did soften a bit. "Never mind . . . I just thought . . ." she stammered.

"You thought what?"

"Jeez, Cooper," Grace sighed. "Would you just relax? It's not like we're strangers."

"We're not?" I blurted.

"You poor thing," she said, shaking her head. Grace was now staring at me like I was some shelter dog about to be put down. Her face was full of pity, something I'd had enough of to last me many lifetimes over. Personally, I would have preferred a punch to the gut any day.

The dots that had been laid out for me finally lined up in my mind. If Blake was my supposed good buddy then it would make sense that Grace and I knew each other.

"So . . . you and Blake? The two of you are together, huh?"

Grace bit her lip and pulled back from me. The butterflies were doing some bad-ass pirouettes in my gut. The idea of the two of them together wasn't sitting right with me, but it wasn't like it was any of my business. The faster I completed Lucy's mission, the faster I could hightail it out of this place.

Of course, I couldn't just leave it at that. I had to push the issue a little further. "So, uh . . . like, is Blake really your kind of guy? I mean, he doesn't strike me as your kind of thing," I said.

"You shouldn't care what my *thing* is, Cooper!" Grace hugged her notebook to her chest and glared at me.

There were those eyes again. Like storm clouds, Grace's gray eyes pelted me with fist-sized hail.

"I can't believe you! All these years and you finally have an opinion. Well, that wasn't part of the arrangement."

"The arrangement? What are you talking about?" I was back to being confused.

Grace shook her head. The anger washed out of her face and she was back to pity. I knew girls could be moody, but Grace was the definition of moody.

Before sending me off on my merry way, Lucy hadn't said anything about asking for directions while I was on this little trip. "Excuse me," I said, "but do you mind shedding a little light on what's going on here?"

Grace's eyes welled up with tears. She opened her mouth, but before she could say another word, Blake came running over. Practice was done.

Blake shifted his glance from me to Grace. "You hitting on my girl, Coopman?" He laughed nervously. His question was followed up with a friendly hit to my shoulder that sent shockwaves of pain clear through my shoulder pads.

Her tears gone now, Grace stood to meet Blake. Her head barely grazed the bottom of his chin as he swallowed her up in a predatory hug.

I'd obviously learned nothing about self-preservation from my previous life, because all I wanted to do was slug the jerk.

With her arms around Blake, Grace said, "Why would I want a scrub like this when I could have a real man like you?"

Any remaining butterflies that had been fighting to take flight were killed by Grace's icy tone.

A horrible thought crossed my mind. Was this what

Lucy wanted? Forget about all that redemption crap, what if Lucy had tossed me into Hell without me knowing?

Blake planted a big sloppy, onion-stenched kiss on Grace. As he did, Grace's fists balled up by her sides. It was just part of the passion, I supposed.

Whatever it was, I was out of there.

CHAPTER 5

△

Since I'd never been too comfortable with the whole communal shower thing, I hung back while everyone else took their turn. I was also purposely trying to avoid Blake. Every time I pictured him kissing Grace, I wanted to plow the football field with his big jock face.

Why did I feel this way? From everything I had seen, Grace's moods turned faster than a New York City subway turnstile. If I was going to make the most of this second chance, there was no point in wasting what little time I had with someone like her. After all, who said I had to follow Lucy's rules? Did I really want to get into Heaven that bad? Maybe Hell was more fun and the people more interesting.

When the showers emptied out, I stripped down. In the afterlife, after you got your personal makeover, you never dirtied up again. As much I tried, my nails stayed manicured and even my breath stayed fresh. As I rubbed the soap over my chest, the bubbly water slid over my shoulders, becoming a river that merged south to my happy zone. It felt good. I looked down at my nails. One of them was chipped and a bit of dirt from the field had gotten lodged in my knuckles. On purpose, I kept that hand out of the stream of water.

Unfortunately, with all that humanness came other

things I would have rather pushed out of my brain, but they refused to go away. The images appeared in my head wide-screened, but with no popcorn. Art house movies that might as well be in French – that was how foreign they felt.

The first played out the way it always did, with a small boy hanging out on a porch with two wood slat chairs. The way the kid picked his nose when he knew no one was watching was familiar. All kids did that, I told myself.

Mrs. Ulip used to say these kinds of fantasies were common, something kids like me needed to help them get through the day. But even here, under the pulse of the shower, I could feel the breeze running through my hair as I took a turn on that tire swing. If these were fantasies, why did they feel so real? As the water turned from warm to cold, I had an irresistible craving for cocoa.

Reaching for a towel, I dried my legs, my arms, and all the parts in between. The Ticklers had done a great job. Every inch that had been burned up and crusted over was now soft and new.

I took my time dressing, but when I was done I was back to square one with nowhere to go. Lucy had set my course so far. She would do it again. At least I hoped. Faith had always been a slippery thing for me.

I wandered out of the locker room and followed a few kids to the front of the school. Pushing down on the door's steel handle, I was blinded by a sharp light. My first thought was that Lucy had changed her mind and pulled the plug on her little experiment. Or maybe Saint Pete had seen enough. And who could blame him? Even I, who didn't know where I was supposed to be going, felt like I was heading smack into nowhere.

My eyes adjusted and I saw that it was just the sun, hanging low in the sky and getting ready to call it a day.

In the parking lot, cars were lined up for pickup. A few parents sat in their vans, but one tall, cocky looking guy was standing outside of his candy-apple red Camaro. Every once in a while, to announce to the world that he was there, he beeped his horn obnoxiously. Some pretty girls by the side of the school ogled the guy hungrily. What a dope. The guy acted like the girls weren't even there.

I'd take a hundred Rastafarian albinos any day to a guy like that who thought his good looks and money gave him the right to act like a creep.

What the rich punk did next nearly knocked me on my ass. He started waving. Not at the girls, but at me!

"Yo! Boomer!" he called to me.

Boomer? There was no way this guy was talking to me.

"Boomer!" he yelled again.

The group of cute girls looked at me and smiled. Lucy had got to be kidding.

As I dragged my feet across the parking lot, Mr. Perfect got in the car and revved up his motor. The groupies back on the sidewalk swooned. No matter what, there was no way I was getting in the car with this creampuff.

As if my decision didn't count anymore, the guy swung open the passenger side door. "Come on, will you? We're already late! Mom and Dad are going to be pissed if we don't get there soon!"

Mom and Dad. To most people the words went together as naturally as peas and carrots and were just about as common. Not me. Curiosity pushed down on me, and before I could think straight, I was sitting in a molded leather seat, racing away from the school.

By the time I regained some of my senses, we were on the highway. For all his complaining, we were barely moving beyond the speed limit. While he drove no faster than a sloth, the creampuff sure could talk. In fact, he didn't shut up. "Mom and Dad have been texting me non-stop. I can't believe it! Do you know how long I've been waiting for you out there? I mean every teacher I ever had was coming up to me, asking me how things were going. Jeez, Boomer! Did you really have to put me through all that? I swear this is the last time I pick you up."

And just in case there was any question, he added, "I mean it!"

As his jabbering went in one ear and out the other, I checked out the car. I started to think the car was Lucy's way of making up for some of her tackier choices. The Camaro was a classic with its leather seats and shiny chrome finishes. The raccoon tail hanging from the rear-view mirror was a little much. The next time creampuff boy wasn't looking, I planned to hurl it out the window.

"Nice," I said when I found that the old eight-track tape in the console still worked.

"Yeah. Very. And if you don't start pitching in with washing it, this plush ride isn't going to be carrying your hide anywhere!"

I shot a sideways glance at the kid. He'd said Mom and Dad were waiting for *us*. The reality that he and I were brothers settled in. Lucy had gotten some of the details right. The guy had the same thin lips as me, but other than that and the fact that we both had ears that were a little too big for the rest of our heads, the resemblance just wasn't there.

Sorry, Luce. You definitely dropped the ball on this one, I thought.

"I can't believe you forgot tonight was Mom and Dad's anniversary dinner," faux-bro said. "I reminded you a million times!"

A million and one times, I was sure, given how compulsive he was about his hair. Every time faux-bro pulled to a stop, he checked himself in the rear-view mirror. Whoever he'd been harping at about tonight's dinner had most definitely not been me, but who had it been? That was just another question I had to add to the list of questions I planned to ask Lucy the next time I saw her.

33

I continued to fuss with the knobs on the eight-track. I found some tapes in the glove compartment. The music, like the car, was classic.

I left my heart in San Francisco . . .

"Would you leave that alone?" Faux-bro smacked my hand away, nixing the music.

"What? You have a problem with Tony Bennett, too?"

Just then a voice sang out from under my seat. *Yo messin' with my head. Yo messin' with my head. Yo, man. Yo, man. Yo messin' with my head!*

What the . . . ?

"Are you going to get that or what?"

"Get what?" I said.

"Your phone, Shit-for-brains," he said.

The rap music started up again. I finally found my cell in my jacket pocket.

Flipping the phone open, I said, "Hello?"

"Hi, honey," a woman's voice on the other side said. "Dad and I are waiting for you guys at the restaurant. How much longer till you get here?"

When I was younger and I didn't think anyone was watching me, I'd pretend to talk to my mother. The mother in my imagination would call to tell me the line at the store was long, so I shouldn't worry. Sometimes when I was really into it, my pretend-mom would tell me not to go to bed before she got home on account of she was bringing me a surprise.

"Cooper?" the woman said again. Now that it was as real as I'd pretended, my tongue sat in my mouth as still as a lizard sunning itself.

"Tell her we're about five minutes away," faux-bro said to me.

"Um . . . We'll be there in about five minutes," I said.

"Great, sweetie. Daddy and I will tell the maître d' to seat us." After she hung up, I stared at the phone, the promise of it messing with my head fulfilled.

When we got to the restaurant, faux-bro was too much of a prince to park his own car, so he handed the key over to the kid working valet. "You get a ding in it, man, and your ass is grass."

When the valet thought faux-bro wasn't looking, he shot him a hard look. When he noticed me looking, his expression turned embarrassed.

Even though it was a pretty special car, I had half a mind to hand the kid a twenty to key the whole side door.

The restaurant turned out to be some upscale place. In addition to the valet parking, the front of the building had large stone columns decorated with tiny, white lights. In the foyer, tucked in an alcove next to the reservation counter, a string quartet played a dreamy kind of music that hypnotized the customers at the bar into having a few extra drinks.

One of the musicians was a harpist, a tiny woman who plucked at the strings with her long fingers. Unlike the other musicians, who were men and dressed in dark suits, the harpist wore a silvery gown. Midway through her song, she looked up at me like she knew me. That was weird. She didn't look like anyone I'd ever seen before.

I considered going over to talk to her. Maybe she knew what I was supposed to do next. Before I could make up my mind, the maître d' said, "This way to your table, sirs."

It wasn't every day someone called me sir. When I didn't move fast enough for his taste, faux-bro yanked on my sleeve.

"Lay off." I jerked my arm back and the maître d' frowned deeply. I was used to people looking down on me, but faux-bro was not used to being black-balled from civilized society the way I was.

"What's with you tonight?" he whispered so the maître d' couldn't hear.

"Nothing," I said loud enough for everyone in the

35

restaurant to hear. This time the maître d' shushed me, but I was loving every minute of watching faux-bro get his undies in a pinch.

The main dining room was enormous, with a giant stone fireplace on one end of the room and a long row of floor to ceiling windows on the other. Chandeliers dripped crystals like stalactites and the place smelled incredible.

A good-looking couple sat near the large windows facing the golf course. The woman that made up half of the couple got to her feet and waved at us. "Ryan! Cooper!" Her hair fell in soft folds at her shoulders, and when she waved, she was still holding her napkin the way princesses in royal courts hold out their handkerchiefs to the strongest and most honorable of knights.

Prince Camaro, aka faux-bro, apparently had a third name. Ryan stepped ahead of me, and as I watched, he leaned down to give the woman a hug.

When it was my turn, I froze.

"I know, I know. You despise all public displays of affection," she said to me. "But can you make just one itsy bitsy exception?"

I laughed nervously, but not for any of the reasons she might have been thinking.

I talked myself through it, telling myself this was just part of the game. Taking a breath, I leaned over and allowed the woman to draw me in. The feeling was different than when I was sitting close to Grace. Instead of working themselves up into a fury, the butterflies now glided around in my stomach in an almost peaceful way.

When she released me, I was sad and relieved all at the same time. Someone else was at the table. He announced his presence by clearing his throat. This had to be Dad.

"Dad" was tall. His breath smelled minty, but not like in that afterlife makeover way. When he hugged Ryan, it was that old-buddy kind of hug that seemed just right for an occasion like this.

When it was my turn, I stiffened up again. Dad didn't seem to notice. He clamped his arms around my shoulders, coming nowhere close to the bone-crushing version Blake had doled out.

As soon as we took our seats, a waiter came around. Dad made a joke about how the restaurant needed to get take-out from another restaurant in order to keep up with the appetite of his two sons. Apparently, this was an old joke because Ryan groaned like he'd heard it all before. Since I was on the fence, I gave a little chuckle.

Dad took it upon himself to order the appetizers. Once the waiter left, Ryan ripped into me. "Sorry we're late. Boomer here was dragging his feet again."

Other than the other foster kids I'd lived with off and on over the years, I didn't know how it felt to have a real brother. It was weird how we fell into a pattern, Ryan razzing me and me staring him down or kicking his ankle when he just wouldn't quit.

"Cut it!" Ryan said, when my last kick to his ankle was particularly hard.

Instead of getting mad, Dad said, "Hey, guys. Can you wait to get home to break something? These glasses cost more than the new set of tires for my pickup."

I looked at Dad. "You mean we're not rich?"

My blurting problem was turning downright pathological.

"No, kiddo," Dad said. "Unfortunately that Swiss bank account I was counting on never came through."

"That's right, Cooper. Don't get used to this, because tomorrow it's back to Hamburger Helper," Mom said.

Dad smiled and gave Mom a little tweak on her nose. "I personally love your Hamburger Helper," he said.

While my new parental units fell into a conversation about the water bill going up, Ryan slathered butter on his roll. With no way of gauging what a real family was like, I just took it all in. While some of the foster parents had given it a fair shake, I'd never returned the favor. Why bother, I always thought, since it wasn't going to last anyway.

When our dinners came, Ryan stole a couple of my French fries. I had to give Lucy kudos again. She'd gotten all the details down. The rest of the family resemblances were pretty good. While Ryan looked more like Dad, I shared Dad's height and his broad shoulders. From Mom I'd "inherited" my fair skin, oval-shaped eyes and rounded cheeks. If things had turned out differently for me the first time around, this wasn't a bad picture of how my life could've been.

Don't get used to it, I told myself. *You're only a tourist with a one way ticket.*

I ate my dessert slowly, trying to make the chocolate cake on my plate last. Mom smiled first at Ryan and then at me. Though it was nice to have a mom who could smile at you like that, all of this sweet stuff was giving me a toothache. I got up and excused myself.

Back in the foyer of the restaurant, the quartet was taking a break from playing. A few of the musicians were hanging out at the bar.

"Excuse me," I said, approaching one of the men. "The woman who was playing the harp. Do you know where she went? I'd kind of like to talk to her."

The man looked at me like I had two heads. "Kid, aren't you a little too young to be drinking?" The other men who had also been playing in the group started laughing. "Do we look like we have a harp player?"

Walking away, I felt confused. I was sure I'd seen her, but this wasn't the place to argue.

When I returned to the table, everyone's expression looked different, a bit more serious.

Sliding back into my seat, I said. "What's up? Did Dad

get the bill?"

When no one laughed, I was afraid I'd blown my cover. Then Mom said, "No. Ryan just told us something your Father and I find a little disturbing, Cooper."

My eyes flicked over to my so-called brother. Ryan was sitting there looking like a worm as he picked at some left-over crumbs on the table cloth. What had the jerk narked me out for? I was seriously starting to think brothers were an extremely overrated commodity.

"Ryan heard a rumor that Blake is dating Grace Sanders," Dad said. He kept his hands wrapped around his cup. Compared to the delicate porcelain, Dad's hands were large, worker's hands. In my former life, I would have picked up on a clue like that right away. Why hadn't I noticed that before? Had death made me soft?

Shifting in my seat, my mind raced back to the conversation Grace and I had had on the bleachers. "Yeah, it's not like it's any of my business," I said, reiterating the message Grace had given me. But even as the words left my lips, they didn't feel right for some reason.

Mom leaned over and cupped her hand over mine and smiled. Her hand was soft, the way a mother's hand should feel. "We're not trying to pry into your business or Blake's business," she said. "It's just that your father and I don't want you to be upset, especially with you and Blake being good friends and the history you have with Grace."

Here she tightened her hand around mine as if she was trying to send all the strength she had out to me.

Grace and I had a history together. Yeah, she'd mentioned something about an arrangement and how we'd been friends. None of it made sense, but whatever I said in response must've put the parental units at ease because they went back to sipping their six dollar cappuccinos.

Ryan stacked sugar cubes to see how high a tower he could make (and I was the immature one here?). While the three of them seemed okay with my answer, the conversation had added a whole slew of questions to my already overflowing bag.

Dad paid the bill, and Ryan went to get his car. Since I'd had more than enough of him already, I decided to ride in faux-dad's pickup. I sat in the middle while my "parents" reminisced about their first date.

"Do you remember that tie you wore?" Mom asked Dad.

"Who could forget it?" Dad said. "It was a clip-on. It fell into my spaghetti when we were eating." Dad lightly elbowed me. "No clip-ons for you, kiddo," he said.

I had to admit it was a pretty funny story, but it was hard to focus, what with a picture swinging from the rear view mirror of me as a little tyke. The pickup hit a pothole and the laminated photo swung like a noose. Two towheaded boys stared back. One of the boys looked older. Ryan, I'd bet. While there was no way I'd posed for the shot, the other kid, the one with the dimple in his left cheek, was me.

Dad palmed the steering wheel. As the pickup leaned into the curve, the photograph taunted me. It was as if I was waving back at myself from some unknown world. It had to be another one of Lucy's tricks.

Dad steered the truck down a tree-lined street. If only there was a way of really knowing truth from fiction. I'd tried to fill in the gaps in my life. But when I'd asked Mrs. Ulip, she'd said my old records had gone missing, and there were just no answers to be had.

Dad turned the truck into an unfamiliar driveway.

"Ah! It's good to be home," Mom said.

When I looked out the window, I couldn't believe my eyes. There in the front yard, hanging from an ancient tree, was my tire swing.

CHAPTER 6

△

The Camaro beat us home. As I got out of the truck, the deep base of a heavy metal song thudded against the shiny red steel.

"Like he can afford to lose a few more brain cells," I said. Even though Ryan couldn't hear me, it felt good to take a crack at him for a change.

Mom and Dad were halfway up the walkway.

"Don't worry," Dad said. "Pretty soon it'll be your turn and you'll understand."

Mom shot me one of those mushy expressions I'd only seen TV mothers make. "Car fumes and perfume. A mother's worst nightmare," she said.

Jeez, if she knew half the stuff I'd done. Still, she seemed like a nice lady so I didn't let on.

Dad went in the house.

"Aren't you coming in?" Mom said to me.

I looked at the front door. The warm light that flickered in the front porch lantern caused my stomach to flip over like a circus dog.

"Naw. It's such a nice night. I think I'll just hang out here for a while."

"Okay, sweetie. But remember you have school tomorrow. Okay?" This time she blew me a kiss, which only made me flinch on the inside.

On both sides of the street, the houses were split levels. Figures I'd get stuck with the one with the tire swing out front. I took a few steps toward the porch and in the dim light, I saw two ladder-back rockers.

"Could you be any less original?" I mumbled up to Lucy in case she was eavesdropping.

I plopped down on one of the rockers and rocked with a mean intensity that could churn butter. How'd she done it? How had Lucy managed to pick my brain? It was what she planned to do with all these juicy tidbits that bothered me. If being a kid in the system had taught me one thing, it was to be on the lookout for anyone messing with your head.

My eyes wandered across the lawn. The moon was full, and the tire looked like a U.F.O. hovering a foot above the patchy lawn. Perfect for an alien like me.

I started to wonder. Nah! That wasn't possible.

Before I could really work out the details of my theory, Ryan exited his mobile dance club. As he did I could have sworn he was checking the bushes for paparazzi. Talk about ego. I was happy he'd finally crawled out of his cave, though, because I had a score to settle with him.

He loped up the path in that cocky, arrogant way guys like him always did. Lucy had had a serious lapse in judgment when she'd chosen this moron for my faux-bro. I used to make guys like him cry.

Shifting to the edge of my chair, I got ready to pounce. Then Ryan did the dorkiest thing. He said, "Sleep tight, Boom," and gave me a hug.

Before I knew what to do next, Ryan went in the house without paying his toll.

What a wuss I was. If rinsing away all my bad bits was Lucy's idea of getting me in shape for Heaven, she could keep it.

I leaned over and gripped the rail. My legs felt wobbly

and weak. I had to get a grip, not only on the rail, but on everything. When I looked up, there it was staring me down again. The mother-ship in all its retreaded glory.

Okay, if Lucy wanted me to take a ride, then I'd take a ride. I hopped the porch rail.

The rope the tire was attached to on three sides was thick and weathered with fiber-like wisps poking out of it. It looked solid enough to hold my weight, though. I pumped my legs and quickly found my rhythm. Hanging my head back, the stars were like tiny pin pricks in the inky sky above me.

"I bet the two of you are laughing your asses off right now, huh?" I asked the sky.

When I didn't get an answer back, I did what came naturally. I waved. Only I used one finger to do it.

I got nothing back. No shooting stars. Not even a grumbly rumble that sounded like someone had ordered the nacho platter for dinner. But if they were watching me, they were laughing for sure. Laughing at me was better than forgetting me completely. Though it wouldn't be the first time I'd gone unnoticed. Only this time the system I was floating around in was the Milky Way.

I flattened out my spine. I saw a small flash, which only turned out to be a low-flying plane. The really strange thing was, the longer I sat on that swing, the more I craved hot cocoa.

The voices inside the house had quieted down. When it sounded like everyone had gone to sleep, I finally worked up the courage to go inside. Touching down over the threshold, my foot found quite possibly the only air pocket hidden under the linoleum.

The air rushed out and . . . *Bbrrrrppp* . . .

Dad called down. "Cooper?"

All the other times I'd snuck into a house, I'd never said a word. This time I was forced to speak up. "Yeah! It's me."

That seemed enough.

Being a split level and the fact that Dad's voice had come from upstairs, I assumed that was where my bedroom was, too. For now, I avoided that part of the house. It definitely wasn't the smallest house I'd ever lived in, but it felt tight in a whole different kind of way.

I decided to do some exploring. The hall led past a living room/dining room combo off to the right, with a kitchen straight ahead. A set of stairs led down to a small family room, so I was probably right about the bedrooms being upstairs. Thinking about the hot cocoa, I went into the kitchen first where a round wood table sat in front of three large windows. Everything was tidy, but all the Post-it notes next to the phone proved that people lived there. A bowl full of bananas sat next to a toaster and a jar of loose screws. The fridge hummed in the silence.

A few years back I'd been picked up for illegal trespassing. Nothing major - just a little shack in the woods that, at the time, I'd had no clue was owned by anyone. I liked to hang out there, until the hunter it belonged to found me and called the cops. As I ran my finger over the knobs on the cabinets, peeking in to each one to see what kind of breakfast food the Wandermans ate, something felt different this time around. It was like I'd been here before. I chalked up the feeling to the fact that I'd lived in so many different houses that this house most likely reminded me of one of those.

I opened the last cabinet. Victory! Inside the Swiss Miss box, I found two envelopes of cocoa. Without bothering to find a cup, I ripped one open and sniffed the sweet powder. In appreciation, the moths performed a little tango in my chest.

Why was I torturing myself? I didn't actually belong here. Before I allowed myself to get too carried away, I replaced the opened envelope in the box and headed for the living room.

Next to the sofa, I found a tall bookcase. Someone in this house was organized. The shelves were lined with photo albums, carefully labeled on the spines by year. I pulled out the one from 2002 and flipped open to the first page. The first pictures were of me and Ryan in a pumpkin patch. The bowl haircuts and chubby cheeks were identical to the picture hanging from Dad's rear view mirror. The expressions on our faces, the way Ryan had his arm tossed over my shoulder, and the keen family resemblance was eerie. Just some fancy computer stuff, I reminded myself. Still, the photos messed with my head in a way I didn't like.

I needed to find a little bit of the old me. I strolled around the living room, checking out all the other shelves. I found some CDs, Barry Manilow, Sinatra – old people stuff. Then I saw it. A sleek little souvenir that had my name written all over it. The iPod was charging in its docking station, just waiting to be pocketed. For kicks, I did just that.

See, Lucy. You can take the boy out of his life, but you can't take the life out of the boy.

The weight of the iPod felt solid in my pocket.

I flipped open another album, this one from seven years ago when the fake me was supposed to be ten. There I was again. My hair was a lot darker in this shot, a slightly shorter cut compared to how I usually wore it. This time, instead of Ryan, some girl was next to me. Her pixie face looked familiar, but in the photo she was looking away from, rather than at, the camera.

When I turned the page, there she was again, only this time she was looking straight into the lens.

It was Grace!

This Grace was different from the Grace that had told me to kiss off that morning. It wasn't just the fact that her hair was the color of butter, but she actually looked approachable, and . . . what was the word I was looking for?

Happy.

Gone were the piercings and the face that could melt steel. Her eyes were still gray, but they sparkled like they had mica sprinkled through them. Instead of her notebook, she was holding a floppy-eared rabbit.

Pulling the photo from its cellophane sleeve, I couldn't believe how Lucy really had thought of everything. The picture was complete with a caption written on the back.

Grace meets Grubs for the first time.

But no matter how good Lucy was at retouching photos, she'd messed up on one thing. Nowhere in that picture did it hint at the pink tornado Grace would grow up to be.

Something bothered me, and I went back into the kitchen. Next to the phone, I'd seen a basket with pens. I took one of the Post-its from the wall and went back to sit on the sofa. Without looking at the picture, I wrote something on the Post-it. The handwriting was identical. What was going on here?

I flipped through the album, and time and time again, I was confronted with pictures of Grace and me. Grace and me hanging out on the porch playing cards. Grace and me eating hot dogs while Dad mugged for the camera in the background. There were loads and loads of pictures just like these.

Magic tricks aside, I just didn't get why Lucy had put it all together. I picked up one of the more recent albums. In this one, I found pictures of me and Mom cheering Ryan on as he ran a race. There were other family-type pictures that, of course, I had no memory of, but there were also no pictures of Grace. Lucy didn't make mistakes like that. She'd already proven that she knew what she was doing.

I remembered Grace on the bleachers that afternoon, telling me to relax, and that we weren't strangers. So if we weren't strangers, what were we?

The difference between fake and real was draining my

brain of everything it had left. Exhausted, I considered going upstairs and finding a bed – my bed. But I was in no mood to play out the whole Goldilocks story, so I picked up another photo album instead.

The one I grabbed was from five years ago, which put me at twelve. Instead of the bad report cards I'd racked up then, there were pictures of school parties. Instead of walking around the yard in juvie hall, there was a picture of me holding a trophy. Grace was back on the scene and there were plenty more pictures of us doing stuff together. In two years, Grace had gone from a pretty ten-year-old girl who loved rabbits to a girl who was starting to turn into a woman. Grace's hair was still long, but she wore it high like those ballerina girls. There was an elegance to her, but unlike those ballet chicks, Grace had curves. In fact, one picture looked like a gallon of Miracle Gro had been poured over her. Though I'd only seen her in a loose top, I could tell Grace was hiding some pretty spectacular curves.

As I pored over the pictures, more and more holes opened up with no logical answers to fill them.

This time it was Mom who called down to me. "Go to bed, Cooper. It's a school night." Through my exhausted haze, her voice sounded ghostly.

My limbs felt like sandbags, but I did what she told me.

CHAPTER 7

△

Clean sheets and a soft mattress make for good dreams. The cute girl I was dreaming of giggled as I nuzzled my face into the soft spot behind her ear.

Giggle means go! But as soon as I maneuvered my hand down the Mason-Dixon line, the dream patrol who gave tickets out for this sort of stuff smacked me on the nose.

I jolted up and rubbed my nose. Wow! Some dreams were so real.

My eyelids were still glued partially shut. Hoping the pretty blonde in my dream could convince the troopers that my maneuvers were fine by her, I fell back into the nice, warm nest of rumpled sheets.

"Boomer!" The voice was gruff. Was the blonde catching a cold? Or maybe this dream was more messed up than I thought.

"Boomer! Get up!" Something hard clocked me on the head this time. Whatever it was landed on my pillow and exuded a vomitous stench.

"Ugh! Road kill!" I bounced out of bed, trying to get away from whatever it was that smelled so bad.

"Ha! Ha!" Someone standing in the shadows of my room said.

The adrenaline coursing through me finally helped me

to match the voice to the face.

"You son-of-a . . . ." Before I could get to Ryan, he was already at my window, pushing the cowboy print curtains to the side. For the second time in twenty-four hours, I was knocked completely blind.

"Get your ass in gear." Ryan picked up the road kill still lying limp on my bed and tossed it at me.

"What the . . . ?" The sneaker landed at my feet.

"Yeah, dufus. It's a sneaker. Now go find the other one and I'll meet you downstairs."

As Ryan left the room, I noticed he was all jocked out in a sweat shirt and shorts.

Fifteen minutes later I was outside, my warm breath making steamy clouds in the cool morning air. "Brrr . . . What about my ankle, Ryan? You know, doctor's orders?"

"Aw, stop pussyfooting around," Ryan said. "Everyone knows you've got to work through an injury. And sleeping in isn't going to get you a scholarship."

Sleeping in! It was friggin' five a.m. At that hour, some of my old friends from the hood were still snug in their cardboard boxes.

Not me. I had to have Super Jock as my brother and personal trainer. I was tempted to tell Ryan my future plans did not include an athletic scholarship, but by the way he and Dad had talked last night about some big race Ryan had set a record in, I knew it was pointless to argue.

We stood on the sidewalk, and Ryan looked me up and down. "When are you going to stop jerking around and get your act together?"

It was bad enough that he'd dragged me out of bed at this hour, but now he was going to lecture me too? I'd only gotten one shoe on at that point. Pissed, I chucked the other stink bomb right at his head. Unfortunately for me, he was too quick and caught it.

"Cut it out, Boomer," he said.

"No, you cut it," I said. "Shouldn't you be in some frat house right now, sleeping off a good buzz?"

I didn't expect the kid to have it in him, but whatever I'd said soured his pretty boy profile. "You're just saying that because you're too much of a pansy to race me."

Calling me a pansy touched on a well-worn nerve.

Well, I'd already proven I liked a little challenge. "Sure. I'll race you." I figured the run might loosen Ryan's mouth up a bit, giving me the 411 on this whole Grace thing. I shoved the sneaker on my foot and off we went.

The only running I'd ever done was running away from cops. While that had conditioned me, my form was definitely not as pretty as Ryan's. Trying to keep up with him, stride by stride, I was probably gulping in air faster than I should have. After five minutes it felt like a whole troupe of circus clowns had formed a pyramid on my chest.

Ryan thought he was all that, so he started barking out ways I could do better. "Remember your breathing techniques. In your nose, out your mouth."

I was tempted to shove my fist up his nose. When I did try it his way, I had to admit, my lungs opened up and the clowns tumbled down.

Ryan loved pointing out the other mistakes I was making. "Land on the middle of your foot and then roll through to the front of your toes. Lower your hands. It's easier to run, and you won't look like such a girl."

Whenever I tried it his way, it worked, of course, but I told myself that the only reason I was listening to Ryan was because, in the end, I'd be able to get through the whole running thing that much faster.

Having to concentrate so hard on my running left me with little energy to ask Ryan questions. When we got back to the house, the sun was completely up and a few of the neighbors were getting in their cars, heading out to work, I supposed. In the daylight, I noticed other things about the Wandermans' house that I hadn't noticed the night before. The shutters sure could have used a new coat of paint, and the lawn looked even worse during the day than it did at night. I laughed at myself for having ever thought these people were livin' large.

"Good job today, Boomer." Ryan patted me on the shoulder.

"Huh? Oh, yeah. Thanks," I said, surprised by the compliment.

Now was as good a time as any to bring up the topic of Grace. Before I could, Ryan said, "Beat you to the shower!"

Jeez! Was everything a race to this guy?

Ryan vaulted over the row of low bushes in front of the house. Exhausted from the long run, I didn't even try to catch up.

When I got in the house, Mom was in the kitchen, standing over a frying pan.

"Hope you're hungry," she said. She was wearing an apron so none of the grease from the bacon she was cooking would splatter onto her blouse. Under the apron, she looked like she was dressed for work.

I gulped down a glass of orange juice and watched her. Growing up, I'd had lots of mothers, but none that ever matched the picture I had in my head. With the way she was humming as she flipped over another slice of bacon in the pan, it was like Lucy had stuck a paint brush in my head and painted a picture. Only, in my head, the mother didn't go to work. She just stayed home and baked brownies all day. Or something like that.

Mom looked at the clock on the microwave. "Ryan!" she called up the stairs. "You're going to be late for work!"

Work? But Ryan was the big-guy-on-campus guy.

Mom dished up the bacon and poured herself another cup of coffee. Instead of sitting down with me like I sort of hoped she would, she leaned against the kitchen counter and frowned. More to herself than to me, she said, "I just can't believe those scholarship people. It's not fair, them taking Ryan's scholarship away from him like that."

The ratty lawn, Mom's work clothes, and now Ryan's scholarship falling through. All those things made me realize for the first time that my second-time-around-family could actually have real life problems.

What it was about those people that made them different I couldn't say, but, unlike other times when I'd just been "passing through," I was surprised that I actually cared.

"Why doesn't he just sell the Camaro?" I said. In my mind, it seemed the most obvious solution to the problem. After all, a sweet old car like that could probably rake in a lot of dough.

Mom put her cup down and looked at me. At first I thought she was going to say that was the dumbest idea she'd ever heard, but the pinched look on her face was replaced by a soft smile.

"Now you know your grandfather left that car to both of you, Cooper," Mom said. "I mean, that's a very nice thing you're offering, sweetie. But even if there wasn't so much history in that car, your brother would never sell it knowing half belongs to you."

Even though I hadn't meant to, somehow I'd come out the hero in this conversation. Still, if it were me, I wouldn't have thought twice about selling.

Mom balled up her apron and tossed it on the counter. Then she reached for her purse. "I've got two of the best boys in the world," she said. When she leaned down to kiss me, she smelled like bacon.

A minute later Ryan was in the kitchen, his hair wet and uncombed. I watched him stuff a piece of toast in his mouth as he simultaneously tried to tuck his shirt into his waistband. "Sorry about the hot water situation, Boomer."

I should have been pissed, but somehow I didn't really sweat it.

Ryan was ready and waiting to drive me to school when I came down the stairs. "Don't tell Mom and Dad," he said. Then he handed me the keys to the Camaro.

This was the second time that morning that something about Ryan surprised me. While I'd never officially gotten my license, I wasn't exactly a virgin when it came to driving. The Camaro handled the curves beautifully, but it was the straightaways that were a real thing of beauty.

"Slow down, will ya," Ryan complained as I hit sixty in a thirty-five mile an hour zone.

The day before I might have ignored him. I would have probably pushed the car even faster, just to see him piss his pants. That day felt different between the two of us for some reason. I was still pissed off at him on account of rolling my butt out of bed so early, but I figured he couldn't afford the ticket, so I did what he wanted and eased up off the gas.

We got to the front of the school and Ryan noticed the time. "Shit! I'm going to be late to the deli," he said.

I couldn't believe it. This guy, who was such a total white-bread jock, a guy who could probably have any girl he wanted and who seemed pretty smart too, worked slicing ham and salami all day? A life like that would have made me nuts.

As if he could read my thoughts, Ryan said, "Life doesn't always work out the way you think, Boomer. Sometimes you've just got to make do. Stay out of trouble, okay?"

I got out of the car and Ryan took off. As I watched the Camaro become a small, red gumball on the horizon, I thought about what Ryan had said. Where had doing the right thing gotten him? Because of the bad economy, Ryan was now forced to work in a deli where he sucked up pickle fumes all day long. No, making do and staying out of trouble might have been Ryan's style, but it wasn't mine.

As I joined the rest of the kids heading up the main entrance to Pace High School, I reminded myself that life was what you made of it, whether it was your first, second or fifth time around.

CHAPTER 8

The night before, I'd found a class schedule taped to the pocket of one of my notebooks.

"Thanks, Luce," I'd said. Of course, she didn't say anything back.

Maybe it was the good night's sleep or all that oxygen pumping through my lungs from the early morning run, but I was ready to tackle the world. After all, it wasn't every day a person got another crack at life. I was determined to make it interesting.

I decided I wasn't going to be anyone's puppet anymore. Instead of following my schedule, I hung out in the hallway, checking out the pretty things swishing by in their cheerleading outfits and wondering what old Saint Pete would do if I turned a few cartwheels right here and now.

A voice whispered in my ear, "Don't do it."

It wasn't every day I had a sexy, female voice and the mouth to go with it that close to my ear. Of course it could be Lucy, but when I turned around, the person standing there was a whole other kind of trouble.

"Oh! It's you," I said. I'd spent half the night convincing myself that whatever it was I was feeling about Grace, it was better to just keep things platonic. But what with the way she was standing so close, the scent of her watermelon lip gloss wafting toward me, my throat went dry and my palms got slick.

Grace must have seen what she was doing to me, because a smile tugged upward on her glistening, fruity lips. "Just go to class, Cooper," she advised.

"What? I wasn't going to do anything. Unless you want to do something with me?" So much for my best resolve, but the way Grace's lips quivered into a semi-smile, like she was actually thinking about it, made me glad I'd taken a chance.

Then, just as quick, Grace's eyes narrowed and she shook her head as if she was trying to shake the sexy little thought she'd been having about us out of her head. "Please, Cooper. Watch yourself." Her tone was tinged with something I didn't quite grasp. For a girl who thought of me as a scrub, I didn't get why she cared.

"Are you checking out my woman again, Coopman?" Just like he'd done the day before, Blake snuck up behind me and slipped his burly arm around my neck. This time, Blake's hold was a teensy bit tighter, enough to cut off the air that should have had an otherwise easy passage between my nose and lungs.

Grace's eyes widened, the pink in her cheeks rushing right out of her, bleaching her face ghostly white. She looked as if she might stick up for me or, at the very least, call someone. Instead, she rolled her eyes and huffed. "You guys are so immature!" Then she took off down the hall.

With Grace gone, I supposed there was no one left to prove his toughness to. Blake deposited me back on the ground like a used tissue.

"Jeez, man!" I said, rubbing my neck. For a guy who was supposed to be dead, I sure could feel the pain. "Why do you have to go all Yo! Rocky! on me whenever Grace and I are near each other? I don't want your girl, man!" Though even I could hear how uncertain I was about that fact.

Blake shrugged. "What can I say? Grace is a freak, but

she's my freak."

"Okay, man. I hear ya," I said. The only problem was that no matter how hard I tried to stay away from Grace, she just always seemed to turn up. And when she did, my head just didn't think straight. Well, not the one on top of my neck, anyway.

A teacher poked his head out of his room. "Shouldn't you boys be in class?" he said.

For the first time in a long time, I was honestly happy for grown-up intervention. I figured a little space between Blake and I would do us some good. As I walked to my first class, Blake continued to stalk me.

At the door leading to my Physics class, I turned around to face him. "I told you, man. From now on, Grace is off limits." I put up my hands, letting Blake know there was no reason to drag this issue out. Admittedly, Grace was hot, but no girl was worth having my butt handed to me on a platter.

Blake looked at me like I was a new fungus he'd just discovered growing between his toes. "Okay, I'm over it," he said. That was when he swept by me and right into my next class.

Since we were the last two in the room, only two desks were left. Blake grabbed the desk by the window, sticking me with the desk with one bum leg.

The Physics teacher, Mr. Klein, looked exactly like what I imagined a Physics teacher to look like. His glasses were thick, and his eyebrows thicker. When he talked, he sounded like he was just a short stone's throw away from a full-on asthma attack.

As Mr. Klein talked about a physicist named Hugh Everett, my mind wandered like it always did whenever someone was trying to teach me something. I started thinking about Grace. What would it feel like to kiss her? But if I did try, who would hand me my head on a platter quicker, Blake or Grace? If Blake snapped, he'd probably get it over with a lot quicker. Grace, on the other hand, would tease out the pain. She might even bite my tongue if I tried to kiss her, though it could be worth it.

"Cooper?"

"Huh?" Without realizing it, I leaned too far forward on my desk and nearly toppled over.

The whole class, with the exception of Blake, laughed.

"So, Cooper? Your opinion on Hugh Everett's theory?" Mr. Klein said.

Looking up at the board, I saw where Mr. Klein had scrawled a whole lot of positive and negative signs and the words *Many Worlds Theory*.

"Um," I said.

A few people behind me snickered, and again I leaned too far forward, narrowly avoiding falling flat on my face.

"Okay, Cooper. I see you're not ready to commit." Mr. Klein was cool. He skipped from person to person. "Anyone?"

"I think it's a pretty cool theory," Blake said.

I looked over toward Blake. Though he was answering Mr. Klein, his gaze was squarely fixed on me.

"When you say that the Multiple Worlds theory is cool, are you saying you agree with it?" Mr. Klein asked Blake.

"Well, I know it sounds crazy. And Hugh Everett got a lot of flak from those other brainiacs he worked with. But, yeah. I think alternate universes could exist. I mean, how do we know that this is all there is? Why can't there be another classroom out there, just like this one, with kids like us in it?"

"Just like you?" Mr. Klein asked. By the tone of his voice, I knew he was trying to get Blake to think. From the funny way Blake was looking at me again, I could tell he was thinking plenty.

"Maybe like us," Blake said. "But even though they may look like us, they may be different, too, you know?"

Just then a shiver wiggled up my spine. Did Blake know something about me?

Other kids weighed in. Most of the time, they talked about what their "other selves" might be doing right then. Some girl said she liked to believe her other self was Emma Watson, and some guy said if he had another self, he hoped he would be playing World of Warcraft at home instead of sitting in a science class.

Mr. Klein tried to reel in the discussion by erasing the board and drawing a complex diagram illustrating how Hugh Everett did an experiment where he bounced atoms around. Mr. Klein sprinkled in terms like wave function collapse, random decay, and quantum decoherence for good measure. While I didn't have the kind of brain that could understand stuff like that, I had no reason to doubt it.

But it wasn't physics that concerned me so much as the way Blake kept looking at me. I'd goofed up a lot since I'd been here, but I should have known Blake and I were in the same Physics class.

Mr. Klein drew another line on the board, this one vertical. "Before Everett's theory, reality had been viewed as a single line. With the Many Worlds theory, reality is multi-branched." Here he attached lines shooting out from the first line he'd drawn. "Reality is like a tree where every possible quantum outcome is not only possible, but realized."

Mr. Klein pointed to each one of the branches he'd just drawn with his chalk. "Each branch is a different reality, a different future to embark on."

Another chance, I thought.

The bell rang. I had a question for Mr. Klein. "Have they proved it?" I said. "The theory, I mean."

"There is strong speculation at the molecular level," Mr. Klein said.

What did that mean? But there was no time to ask Mr.

Klein anything else. Blake was waiting at the door for me, and I figured I'd better start acting more like "myself" before it caused me problems.

"So what do you think?" Blake asked me. "Should they start fitting Mr. Klein for his straitjacket?"

"The way you were talking, I thought you believed all that stuff."

"Me? No. I just act all interested so the guy gives me a better grade," Blake said.

Looking at Blake's smug smile, I didn't know whether to believe him or not.

"What about you? Do you think people exist somewhere else?" Blake said. There it was again, that hint of something like he didn't completely trust me. That time though, not having Blake trust in who I was felt like a bigger threat than I could handle.

Sweeping the real me under the rug, I pandered to Blake's ego. "Are you kidding?" I said. "When they made you, they broke the mold."

At least for now, Blake looked like he accepted my answer. Still, the threat felt very real.

After Physics came Calculus, lunch, Spanish, then History, Health, and Art. All of them were Honors classes which royally pissed me off. If I had to be in school again, why couldn't I just breeze my way through? The only good thing about my schedule was that Blake and I didn't share anymore classes for the day. With the exception of English, neither did Grace and I.

I did see her at lunch, though. As soon as I walked into the noisy cafeteria, there she was, sitting alone at one of the long tables near the double doors that led outside. As usual, she was writing in her notebook. Blake was over at the jock table, where someone should have posted a *Sperm Bank for Dummies* sign.

I took myself and the bagged lunch Mom had handed

me that morning and avoided Blake and his crew.

"Mind if I sit here?" I said, pointing to the empty chair opposite Grace.

Over the top of her notebook, Grace's eyebrows moved ever so slightly. She glanced over in the direction of Blake. Then she made a small gesture I took as a yes.

When I unwrapped my sandwich, a foul stench poured out of the tin foil.

Grace popped up from behind her notebook. I was sure she was going to give me grief about the smell. But instead, she said, "Is that Nancy's tuna salad?"

"Nancy?" I said.

"You know, your mom?" Grace looked at me like I didn't have two good brain cells to rub together. And why wouldn't she? What dumbass didn't know his own mother's name?

"Oh, yeah, yeah," I said. In an attempt to not make myself look so stupid, I said, "Do you want half?"

Grace surprised me when she reached out for half of my putrid lunch.

"You like it?" I said, watching her as she downed the half sandwich in just under a minute. I offered Grace the other half and she polished that off as well.

Grace smiled, revealing a little piece of bread crumb on her tooth.

"Um . . . You've got something on your uh . . ." I pointed to her mouth.

Grace fished the crumb off of her tooth with her tongue. "You never did like your mom's tuna salad," she said.

Strange that Grace obviously knew stuff about me I didn't know about myself. Thinking that it might be a chance to get to know her, I asked, "So what are some of the other things I don't like?"

At first I didn't think she would fall for it. But like the other times, she let me in.

"Well, you hate beets," she said.

"That's too obvious," I countered. "Everyone hates beets."

Grace wrinkled her nose like she was thinking. "You don't like hot days on account of your knees sweat!"

"Well, that's just plain weird," I said, not admitting it was true. But didn't most people get clammy behind the knees when it went above eighty?

"Okay, so tell me something I really hate. Something only you would know about me," I said, pressing her.

"You don't like to be alone in the dark. And you still sleep with a nightlight. And you used to have a nightlight in the shape of a unicorn. It was from your Grandma Betty. Ryan broke it, and you made your mother find you one on eBay that looked just like it," she said.

The Dorito I'd just been chewing on suddenly lodged in my throat and I started choking.

"Are you okay?" Grace said.

The Boy Scout next to me looked excited. He shifted in his chair, like at any moment he was going to give me the Heimlich maneuver.

The Dorito dislodged and I waved the kid away. "Sorry. You'll have to get your merit badge some other time."

When I turned around, the concern on Grace's face was marked by disgust.

"Was that necessary?" she asked. "He was only trying to help."

"I can't help myself!" I hadn't meant to snap, but the truth was I didn't like sleeping without a nightlight. And though I had no memory of ever having had a Grandma Betty, the way Grace had talked about the whole nightlight incident felt too real.

After that, it just wasn't worth it. The idea of eating grossed me out, so I played Tiddly Winks with my leftover Doritos. It wasn't like I wasn't aware of Grace's presence.

Actually, it took all I had to ignore her. The more time I spent near her, the harder it was to pull back.

When lunch was over, Grace quickly packed up her stuff and left. As the cafeteria emptied out, a vacuum settled down around me. The emptiness I felt was familiar. I'd felt it my whole life. Not even the fire had managed to fill up the void. But the emptiness at seeing Grace go was different in a way I couldn't explain.

My foul mood followed me to Spanish, which came after lunch. One of my best buddies from the old days had been a kid named Javier. Javier and I liked to go downtown together, where I taught him everything I knew about shoplifting, and he schooled me in the fine art of Spanish street slang.

"Don't be such a *pendejo*," I told the kid in front of me.

I watched as the teacher, Mrs. Salamante, used her red pen to write something in her grade book. I didn't care. It felt good to be a little bad ass.

When it came to English, I didn't know what to do. Grace was already sitting. Like Blake, she had an affinity for the window seat. Reminding myself that I was here on the authority of the Council, I decided to bite the bullet and head for the desk directly next to her.

I'd just made it past Mr. Reynolds' desk when Jimmy grabbed me by the arm. "Dude, I gotta show you something."

Reluctantly, I sat down in the empty desk next to Jimmy. The jock had some new plays he wanted to run by me. No one had told me, but apparently when my ankle wasn't twisted, I was a pretty good running back.

Mr. Reynolds walked in, taking his spot at the podium next to his desk. The day before, my mind had been so cluttered with other stuff that I hadn't noticed the drawing of Shakespeare's head that decorated the front of the podium. The old guy's droopy eyelids gave the impression that even

Shakespeare himself found Mr. Reynolds boring.

Mr. Reynolds cleared his throat. "Yesterday we were talking about how Edgar disguises himself as a beggar and calls himself Old Tom. Some scholars believe that by doing this, Lear, in his observation of Old Tom, is coming to terms with a part of himself that he, until that point, did not want to face. His more honest self."

What bullshit, I thought. I glanced over at Grace. As usual, she was busy scribbling away. Did she honestly like this crap?

Mr. Reynolds reached for the briefcase sitting on the top of his desk. "Since Shakespeare meant for his works to be acted out, our class is going to put on a little production," he said.

"You mean we have to get on stage?" Jimmy asked, incredulously.

"No, nothing that lofty," Mr. Reynolds said. "But some of Miss Lytle's class may come and join us. Since there are many scenes, and you're all a far cry from professional thespians, I am going to divide you into groups, starting with Act 1, Scene 1."

A real brown-noser of a girl named Jaimie Honnaman shot up her hand. "Can I play Cordelia?"

"We're going to do this the democratic way, Miss Honnaman," Mr. Reynolds said. "Everyone, please write your name down on a slip of paper."

When we were done, Mr. Reynolds collected the pieces of paper in his briefcase.

Back up at the podium, he rifled through the papers. "So for Act 1, Scene 1, the part of Gloucester goes to . . ."

He picked out a slip. "Mr. Richards!"

As if the burrito he'd eaten for lunch was making a comeback, Jimmy groaned.

"Miss Icuzzi, you get the part of King Lear's daughter, Regan."

When Jaimie Honnaman got the part of Lear's second daughter, Goneril, someone snickered and called her gonorrhea.

"For the part of the poor, misunderstood daughter, Cordelia, Miss Sanders," Mr. Reynolds said.

Grace stared blankly ahead. If nothing else, we had our dislike of Shakespeare in common.

As Mr. Reynolds blathered on, I tried to figure out what else the two of us had in common. What was this connection I felt every time I got close to Grace? I was starting to think this was way more than just a physical thing. As for the problem Lucy had sent me down here to fix, I could see plenty of problems, but no solutions. There had to be more to it.

While Mr. Reynolds picked out more names, my eyes wandered down to his shoes. Were those silver socks he was wearing? Remembering what Grace had said about Mr. Reynolds wearing tights under his pants, I couldn't help but laugh.

"Care to share your joke with the rest of us, Mr. Wanderman?" Mr. Reynolds asked.

"Nope," I said. When I looked down again, Mr. Reynolds' socks were plain black. Was I losing my mind?

Reynolds pulled out the last piece of paper. "And for the most coveted role of all," he said "The part of King Lear goes to . . . Ah! Mr. Wanderman."

"Crap!" I said, under my breath. Mr. Reynolds smiled smugly.

With the parts divvied up for the first act, Mr. Reynolds handed out a bundle of papers to the people who'd been chosen for roles. "Since it's not feasible for your generation to memorize the entire act, I've taken it upon myself to piece together and edit the more salient points," he said.

Leafing through the pages I'd just been handed, I still didn't understand. Before I could figure it out, the bell rang.

"As for the rest of you, don't worry," Mr. Reynolds said, thumping on his briefcase. "We'll get to you tomorrow."

People streamed toward the door, but one question remained. If I hadn't written anything down on my piece of paper, how had Mr. Reynolds picked me?

CHAPTER 9

The next day, there was Ryan, standing over my bed the same way he'd done the day before.

"Let's go," he said.

Groaning, I turned over. The night before, Mom had baked cookies and I'd snuck a few up to my bed. Even though I could feel cookie crumbs in my sheets, there was no way I was leaving a nice, warm bed to go running with steroid boy.

"Come on, Boomer. Stop being such a Twinkie." Ryan yanked the pillow out from under my head.

I groaned some more, but this time it was because I knew Ryan was right. I was turning soft. This cushy life was nice, but I better not get too used to it. Reluctantly, I rolled out of bed. A few minutes later I was outside, my warm breath making smoke signals in the air.

Overnight my muscles had tightened up. As I tried to keep pace with Ryan, the sand I'd felt in my legs the day before had turned to concrete.

Up ahead, Ryan turned to look at me. "Pick up your speed!" He was now running backwards.

The air shot out of my lungs faster than I could get more in. As I tried to keep up, I noticed Ryan's stride. As quick as one foot stepped down to the ground, the other foot rose up, as if he was floating. Life came easy to someone like Ryan. Someday, when Ryan passed on, he'd make it right into heaven with no problem.

We were following a different route today. My lungs were tight against my chest, and I felt drunk from all the oxygen circulating through my brain. When I saw the dip in the road, I was relieved. Gravity was finally on my side. I hit my stride, my legs falling into a smooth rhythm and my arms pumping gently, just the way Ryan had told me to. The heaviness in my chest lightened, and I actually started to like the way the cool air felt against my face.

"Don't get used to it," Ryan said. "Remember, we have to go back up."

Talk about a kill joy. Okay, so he spent most of his day fishing pickles out of a barrel, but I didn't think it was right that he pissed in other people's cornflakes.

The road dead-ended. The houses on either side of the street came to an abrupt halt where a large wooded area was visible. Not thrilled with the idea of having to make it back up the hill, I came to a stop.

"Don't stop now. You'll regret it," Ryan said, as he continued to jog in place.

"Is that a path?" I pointed to a spot near the trees where the ground looked worn down. A nice, flat path was definitely a better alternative than going up that damned hill. It was then that I saw the dew sprinkled on the bushes, and I heard a delicate chime ring out. "What was that?" I asked, kneeling down.

Ryan looked at me like I was weird. "Are you okay?" he asked.

The air was still, but I could have sworn the branches on the trees were curling up, like fingers waving me closer.

"Yeah. I'm fine. I just thought . . ." I looked at the woods again. This time I noticed the *No Trespassing* sign sunk into the ground. I'd missed it the first time, most likely because it was hidden behind some overgrown bushes.

"You're sure you're okay?" The expression on Ryan's face tipped me off that I was teetering on the edge of giving myself up. As good as Lucy's trick was, I still got the sense the trick had some rules attached to it that I hadn't yet been able to decipher.

Covering my tracks, I said, "That! Over there. Was that a raccoon?"

Ryan leaned down trying to peer through the bushes. "I don't see anything."

"No? Oh, well. It must have taken off," I said, happy that he'd bought my excuse.

"Come on. Those things aren't supposed to be outside during the day. It might have rabies." Ryan picked up his pace and started back up the hill.

Exhausted, I willed my legs to start pumping, but the uphill trudge was worse than I imagined. Worse yet was the chiming I still heard in my ears. It was as intoxicating as Lucy's perfume, and it drew me in.

Ryan, who only talked during his run to correct my form, must have seen me struggling. "Stay away from those woods, Boomer. You remember what happened to you the last time."

I couldn't explain why, but Ryan's warning sent a chill down my spine. The coldness mingled with the sweat my body was producing. The butterflies must have felt it, too. They beat their wings, as if demanding to be let free.

With each step, I felt a little stronger, and the ringing sound waned. When we were finally outside our house, I leaned forward with my hands on my knees. The smell of pine, the ring of the chime, the way the dew sat on the leaves, all of it felt as heavy as sadness. Those things pressed against my skin. I had to fight the urge to turn around and go back.

It was Ryan who helped me shake off the weird cocktail of feelings swirling around inside of me. He put his hand on my shoulder and said, "You better get going or you'll be late."

I nodded, but didn't say a word. It was the first time since landing there that I was actually glad to have Ryan for a big brother.

Later, as I stood in the shower, my skin still tingled from what I'd experienced. The last time I'd been so freaked out was the day of the fire.

That day, as I'd piled the rags in a long line up against the door, sealing the thin space between the door and the floor, I'd been worried my plan wouldn't work. I pretty much sucked at everything else. Why would that be any different?

The smell of the gas was oily, exotic, but when I struck the first match, it didn't light. What kind of a-hole can't even light a match? That was when I got up and started pacing the room.

What was I doing there? Was it really what I wanted? The problem was I didn't know what I wanted. The anger had been building inside of me for so long, I needed to siphon some off somehow. But what about the kids who had to come to school on Monday morning? What would they think when they saw their school totally trashed? And what about the teachers who might lose their jobs on account of me? Or the crossing guards? With no school, there wasn't any need for them, either. Mainly, I thought about the Rasta albino guy who'd called me names. Even if I made the front page of the Daily News, I bet he didn't even read the paper. I was starting to have major doubts.

The smell was what finally pulled me out of all of that self-loathing. The smell was the same as when people in the neighborhood start firing up their barbecues for the first time of the season. When I turned around, the first rag in line was smoldering and there was a quick flick of orange, as, one by one, all the other rags caught.

Like the idiot I was, I started stomping at the rags with my foot. That caused my pant leg to catch fire. Completely forgetting the stop, drop and roll technique, I pounded at my pants with my hands. My distraction only gave the rest of the fire a nice little head start. By the time I knew it, the rags were all but incinerated, and the fire was climbing up a wall of cardboard boxes I hadn't noticed before. The boxes were stacked one on top of the other, making for perfect kindling.

Pressing my eyelids tight, I resisted remembering what came next. The pain was excruciating, only made worse by the fact that I'd brought it all upon myself.

Turning off the water, I reached for a towel and dried off. It was strange to be comparing what had happened in the fire to what I'd experienced earlier this morning. While one was real, I'd clearly imagined the other, but somehow the two things felt connected.

Just like the morning before, Ryan let me drive the Camaro. Zipping around in that sweet ride helped to clear my mind, if only just a little.

The first part of the day passed slowly. In Physics we had a sub. While everyone else was working on a worksheet, I flipped through my text book and read up some more on Hugh Everett and his theory of multiple worlds. I'd already seen the afterlife and Earth, and I knew that both Heaven and Hell existed. Beyond that, how many worlds were there?

Blake wasn't at lunch, and even Grace was a no show. The two of them were probably somewhere doing something I would probably never have a chance to do. I spent the rest of lunch burrowing holes into my sandwich, pretending the oozing jelly was Blake's brain goo.

It wasn't until English that Grace finally appeared. Mr. Reynolds sent us to the Media Center to work on our parts. As I walked down the hall, Grace walked ahead. The other girls ignored her. Was it because of the way she dressed? She was wearing a skirt that flounced around her knees when she walked. While her fashion sense was definitely a little out there, there was no other reason I could see for the other girls to stay away other than jealousy. Even with that hair and heavy eyeliner, Grace was a standout.

Every time I tried talking to her, she zoomed ahead as if she were purposely trying to avoid me.

The Media Center was a big room with a lot of little rooms located inside of it. These rooms were called silent rooms though, ironically, that's where we were allowed to be as loud as we wanted. Each group took a room.

"Would you concentrate on your lines!" Jaimie yelled at Jimmy, who was more interested in studying his play book than doing his part.

Grace was watching me, but when I tried to catch her gaze, she quickly looked down.

Jaimie, who was determined that the rest of us would ruin her stellar GPA, took charge. "Let's just go over the plot again to figure out who is who, who loves who and who hates who," she said.

The way Jaimie said this made King Lear sound simple, like the soap operas one of my foster mothers used to watch.

"The way the story goes, King Lear is an old king who is tired of ruling," Jaimie said. "He decides to divide his kingdom, divvying it up between his three daughters. Being all kingly and full of himself, Lear decides to make it into a little contest, asking each one of his daughters to tell him how much she loves him. But when Cordelia, his youngest and most favorite daughter, refuses to play along, Lear gets pissed and disowns her."

"I don't get it," I said. "Why doesn't Cordelia just blow sunshine up the old man's skirt the way her sisters do?"

"What? Just so she can get some land?" Grace said. She'd been sitting there looking like she'd rather be hanging out in an airport bathroom than talking about King Lear. But something about the conversation had sparked her, the spark igniting a fire that showed through her eyes.

The rest of them, Jaimie included, must have seen it too. They looked at Grace warily, like people who were too afraid to get close. Good or bad, I'd already proven in one lifetime that fire attracted me.

"Yeah," I said, trying to pull Grace in. "Why shouldn't she just tell him what he wants to hear so she can get what she wants?" Grace shook her head. At first I thought she was laughing, but there was a heavy dose of sarcasm in her words. "You just don't get it, do you?"

"What am I supposed to get?" I asked. My question was really two questions wrapped in one. Maybe this was it. Maybe Grace was going to be the one who was finally going to let me know what I was supposed to do to earn my way into Heaven.

But Grace was not obliging. "What you don't get, Cooper, is that everything comes with strings attached. Every deal we make. It's complicated."

Grace's eyes remained fixed on me longer than she'd ever allowed. Woodstock erupted inside of me, and the butterflies wore peace signs on their breasts and tiny mud boots on their tiny insect feet as they trudged through the sea of mud and love.

"Are we still talking about the play?" Jimmy said.

Okay, so it wasn't just me. Even a dope like Jimmy could feel the shift in the vibe Grace was sending out.

Usually, I wasn't into this kind of debating, but this was the closest Grace and I had come to having a real conversation. I wasn't about to let it slide. "If Cordelia loves King Lear then why doesn't she just tell him?"

"If she loves him, why does she need to tell him? Shouldn't he just feel it?" Grace asked.

Though she was plenty far from me, Grace's words slapped me in the face. Shouldn't he just feel the love she was sending him? Yes, yes. He did. Didn't he?

Before I could fully absorb what this meant, Jaimie suggested we go over our lines together.

The kid who was playing Edmund, whose name I could not remember for the life of me, was asking Jaimie all sorts of questions I only half listened to. My mind felt like a soggy piece of bread, trying to absorb everything that had been dumped on it. Had Grace, in a roundabout way, just declared her love for me? But was she declaring her love for me or for the Cooper she had once been friends with, the Cooper who had lived the life photographed, developed, and filed neatly into all of Nancy Wanderman's photo albums?

Like running in the morning with Ryan, my heart was going at a much faster speed than my brain. The bigger question was who did I want Grace to be in love with?

Kid-Edmund was bound and determined to interrupt my thoughts. "What the heck is this supposed to mean?" he said. He read from a bit of his part. "I should have been that I am, had the maidenliest star in the firmament twinkled on my bastardizing."

"Well you are kind of a bastard." Jimmy laughed. "Maybe Mr. Reynolds just figured you were perfect for the part."

I couldn't help but agree.

Grace, for some reason, thought that Kid-Edmund deserved to have a little light shed on his ignorance. "What Edmund means is that nobody's destiny is planned out for them," she explained. "That's what he means when he says 'I should have been that I am.'"

"But what's all this crap about bastardizing?" Kid-Edmund asked again.

"I know! I know!" Jaimie said, acting all teacherly. "In the play, Edmund is an actual bastard since he's Gloucester's illegitimate son. But what he is saying in those lines is that people get what they deserve."

Grace nodded in agreement.

This time I held my tongue, but I still wondered. Did she honestly believe we all got what we deserved? If that was true, then what were my chances?

Grace tipped her head back and looked up at the ceiling. With her metal hooped earrings glittering in her ears, she reminded me of a gypsy. Instead of reading tea leaves though, she seemed to be eking out the meaning of life from the ceiling tiles. Grace's neck was long, a small hollow formed at the base of it. Had the other Cooper ever kissed that spot? If he hadn't gone for it, he was more of a wuss than I thought.

"Hey, Coop. You okay, man?" Jimmy said.

The room suddenly turned very warm. The bell had rung without my realizing it, and everyone was packing up their stuff to go.

Of course, I couldn't just run after her. I watched, feeling not a little helpless as Grace reached the door before the rest of the crowd and disappeared.

Jimmy waited around, but I told him to go, pretending I had to look for a book in the library. He threw me a funny look, but then shrugged. "See you at practice, then," he said, before leaving.

The silent room was finally living up to its name. The silence closed in on me, and I was close to screaming. What was I supposed to do with all these new feelings inside of me?

I kicked something. When I looked down, I recognized Grace's notebook immediately. Picking it up, I half expected Grace to come charging through the door to reclaim it. She didn't. Opening that notebook felt as intimate an act as looking through Grace's underwear drawer would be. Flipping through it, I was amazed. There were more than a few ink smudges from where Grace had pressed too hard against the paper. Her handwriting was big and loopy, many of the words falling off the page completely as if she'd been in a rush to write them. But they weren't words. I was no expert in languages, but from what I could tell it was just a lot of gibberish.

In one of the group homes I'd lived at, I'd met a kid who'd made up his own language. That kid was off his rocker and they let him write like that just so he wouldn't flood the toilets. Flipping through the notebook again, it hit me that Grace was writing in code. Realizing those pages might give me some real clues about who Grace really was, I tucked the notebook in my pack and headed home.

CHAPTER 10

That night Dad fired up the barbecue and Mom set the plastic plates on the patio table out back. When Mom put the last dish in place, she tilted her head back and smiled. "Just smell that air!"

"Enjoy it while you can," Dad said. He flipped a burger over on the grill. "Before you know it, it'll be winter."

I sat at the wooden picnic bench ticking off the days in my head. Three days had passed already, and I was no closer to figuring out how I was supposed to redeem myself.

Mom was right. The early autumn air smelled great. I'd heard there were no seasons in Heaven. Everything was changeless and flat. Kind of like Florida.

Ryan was sitting across from me, eating gobs of potato salad right out of the container. The sun was hovering just above the horizon. A thin strip of light was all we had to eat by, but it was enough for me to see the mess of mayonnaise Ryan was getting on his shirt.

"Can you eat like a human, please?" My disgust was obvious.

When Mom and Dad were looking the other way, Ryan flipped me the bird.

"Real original response, dufus," I said back. But I said it low enough so the parental units wouldn't hear. The two of them looked kind of happy together, hovering over the barbecue, poking at the beef patties to see if they had any moo left in them.

Looking around at the backyard with its sagging fence and the shed that was in sore need of a paint job, I realized the Wandermans' life was far from perfect, but it was real.

Dad brought over a platter of burgers and Ryan grabbed one. "Bet you can't make a better burger than me." He started piling on cheese, pickles, relish, ketchup.

Normally, I wouldn't take such a stupid bet. But since I liked an easy win, I said, "You're on!"

To my burger I added pickles, onions, jalapenos, extra cheese, ketchup and mustard. By the time I was done, my dinner looked like the Leaning Tower of Glopville.

"Okay, now let me see if you can get that big mouth of yours around it," Ryan said.

Making my burger wasn't half as fun as eating it. Though most of it slid down my chin and onto my shirt, the burger was delicious.

Mom lit a lantern for some extra light, and the crickets came out and sang.

"You guys are goofballs," Dad said.

Mom was sitting next to me. She said, "You goofballs will be doing your own laundry." Then she leaned in and kissed me on the cheek.

"Aw! Mama's boy," Ryan teased.

Another unoriginal crack from Ryan, but this time the hairs on the back of my neck shot up straight.

"Shut up!" I slammed my fist down so hard it made the pickles slosh in their jar.

"Cooper!" Dad's voice was a whole octave deeper when he spoke.

Mom put her hand on my shoulder. When she did, it had the same effect Ryan's hand had had on me that morning.

"Apologize to your brother, Ryan," Mom said. "You

too, Cooper."

The two of us nodded at each other in a begrudging kind of way.

"Come on, guys. Stop the horsing around and finish up," Dad said, but his expression had changed, and he was looking at me in a different way than he had before.

Mom and Dad went back to talking about their day at work, and Ryan finished up the last bit of potato salad. As the few beads of sunlight disappeared completely, my mood sank, too. From what I'd seen of Ryan, I knew it wouldn't take him long to get over it. So why was it so impossible for me to let things go? Why did I always have to react?

I excused myself, throwing my dish out before heading up to my room. Grace's notebook sat on my desk. I'd been trying to decipher its strange language ever since I'd gotten home that afternoon.

I flipped the notebook open. Grace dated all her entries. The entry I was trying to decode was from two years ago. According to what I'd pieced together from both Ryan's comments and the photos I'd found in Mom's albums, this would have been around the time when Grace and I had stopped being friends.

Ubevuben thubough Ubim nubot dubead Ubi mubight ubias wubiell bubie. Thubis prubomubisube ubis kubillubing mube.

Who, besides some dweebie second grader, would go through the trouble of making up a secret code? Grace, that was who.

I pulled open the top drawer to my desk. It was well stocked with pads of paper in different sizes. The pens, which sat in a little tray made specifically for them, were also neat and sorted by color. It wasn't just the desk that was anal and uptight. The closet was also sorted by color and category depending on whether or not the shirt was button-down, crew-neck or a T-shirt. The whole room screamed loser with its trophies and certificates of achievement.

Then I remembered that loser was me. How Lucy had masterminded her whole scheme was a question I'd have to ask once I got back to the afterlife.

I rewrote Grace's code down on a clean sheet of paper. Then I read it out loud to see if that helped. The only thing it did was give my tongue a good workout.

I started thinking. Maybe I wasn't the first one Lucy had ever done this little experiment on. If Lucy got a kick out of sending me back, there was a possibility other people had gone before me, maybe even Grace.

My imagination was out of control, and the all-too-perfect room was starting to get to me.

"I'm going out for a run," I told Mom and Dad. They were sitting in the family room with the lights out. The glow from the TV almost made them look like mannequins who were posed to look like a mother and a father. "Remember, not too late," Dad said.

With all the running I'd been doing, walking now seemed too slow, and I started jogging. While my legs were still sore, after a couple of blocks, my muscles limbered up, and I was pleased at the light pace I could maintain.

My breathing kicked into a steady rhythm, and it was enough to clear my head. Without consciously thinking about it, I followed the route Ryan and I had taken that morning. When I got to the dead end, I stopped. There it was again. The *No Trespassing* sign.

From here, the sky looked flattened out, wider, as compared to the cramped-up sky visible from the Wandermans' backyard. The houses here were more spread out from each other. That could be the reason the sky looked different and why the moonlight was bright enough for me to see the path of crushed pine needles. A scrubby tree was the only thing masking the entrance.

A familiar tinkling sound reached my ears. The chiming

noise was the same one I'd heard that morning. I swung my head around. The sound had to be coming from one of the houses. People liked to hang wind chimes in their gardens.

The chime tinkled again, and I swung my head back around. There was no question. The sound was coming from inside the woods.

I took a step forward, and, as if it was pleased, the chime morphed into a giggle. "Lucy?"

The giggle fanned out and pulled me to it. The butterflies erupted in response, but I didn't know if they were beating their wings to push me forward or hold me back.

"Lucy? Is that you?" I asked again. The only response I got was another giggle.

Remembering Ryan's warning, I hesitated. According to him, something bad had happened in those woods. Then again, what was bad in Ryan's mind was not necessarily bad to me. What? Had the other Cooper Wanderman fallen over some exposed tree roots and ripped a hole in his pants? For the other Cooper Wanderman that would have been a tragedy. Not for me.

I heard the giggle again. I'd know Lucy's seductive laugh anywhere. This was my chance to ask her some questions, and I was going to take it.

Ignoring the pounding in my chest, I moved forward.

For a path that wasn't supposed to be well-traveled, I was surprised by how flat and soft the dirt under my feet was. Above me some kind of animal was making a screetchy, chittering noise. I pulled up my collar. As if it knew I was following it, the giggle chimed in my ear. The path flowed straight through to a clearing. The trees were sparser around the rim of that tract of land, making the night sky visible again. Looking up, I saw pinpoints of light miles away. Would Lucy beam herself down to meet me?

I stood there waiting. The breeze picked up and the cold air snuck beneath my upturned collar.

"Lucy?" I called, peering into the bushes. When I got no response, I wondered if I'd made a mistake in not listening to Ryan. My mind lurched back to Dad and Mom back home on the couch. While they might not be my real parents, they viewed me as their son. How soon before the Wandermans sent out the National Guard to look for their precious kid?

I decided to head back. When I turned around, I saw not one but two paths before me.

Even I wasn't beyond seeing the irony in this situation. "Okay, Luce," I said, talking to the sky. "It's obvious you wanted me to come here, but don't you think this whole 'fork in the road' thing is a little predictable? Even for you?"

Though I didn't want to admit it to myself, I'd kind of been hoping for another giggle. Instead, I heard a growl. Swinging around, I saw something high in the dark trees, two beady, red eyes glaring down at me from the shadows. Another snarl, and I didn't have to think twice. I grabbed a broken branch from the ground and got ready to defend myself. Even with my limited knowledge of small, fuzzy, woodland creatures, my gut told me this was no raccoon.

Another snarl, this time followed by a bolt of white, hot light aimed at my feet. I jumped out of the way just in time. Now that my feet were in motion, they didn't stop. If this was Lucy's way of making up my mind quickly, she got her way. Without hesitation, I quickly chose a path and kept going.

The adrenaline rush shot me out of those woods in no time. Before I knew it, I was back out on the street. With no intention of hanging around a second longer to see if the creature would follow me, I started for home.

Damn! Where was I? Sure, the houses looked pretty similar to the ones in my neighborhood, but I was obviously in a different part of town. The street signs gave me no clues as to what direction I should turn.

There was no way I was going back in those woods, and I was seriously considering knocking on someone's door when I saw a car making its way down the road. The car stopped in front of a lamppost a couple of houses up from where I was standing. Thinking I could ask these people for directions, I started walking toward the car, but then I stopped. Someone, a girl, rushed out of the passenger side. The lamplight illuminated her enough to see that as she stalked up the driveway, she was holding her arm tightly against her like she was hurt or trying to protect herself. From the driver's side, a big, burly guy bolted out of the car. He, too, stalked up the driveway, catching the girl by her arm before she could make it to her front door. The couple started yelling and screaming at each other, and then the big guy raised his hand, swinging it down across the girl's face.

I flinched.

A new supply of adrenaline burst into my blood stream, and I rushed forward to help the girl. But it was far enough and the guy fast enough that, by the time I got within a few yards of the girl's house, he was already in his car, barreling straight for me.

Though I was technically dead, I wasn't taking any chances. I jumped out of the way of the speeding car, rolling myself right into the gutter.

By the time I picked myself up, the girl was gone and the porch light on her house turned off. From the street, I stood in front of her house and stared. Part of me wanted to knock on the door to check how she was doing, but part of me said I should just leave it be. After all, no one had ever stood up for me.

I was about to go when I noticed the mailbox with its red flag still raised on the side. Opening up the box, I found the electric bill all made out and ready to go for when the postman came in the morning. Given all the things that had happened to me that night, reading the name on the return

address on that envelope shouldn't have surprised me.
      But it did.

CHAPTER II

It was all starting to add up. Lucy's luring me into the woods, scaring me onto the other path, then me finding that envelope in Grace's mailbox. I finally got it. The reason I was here. My job was to help Grace get away from that asshole, Blake. The only problem was, would Grace let me help her? The girl had already proven she could run hot or cold depending on which way the wind was blowing. Once I thought about it, I realized she was at her weirdest whenever Blake was around doing his little jealousy routine.

I made up my mind to try, not just for Heaven's sake, but because nobody should be tossed around like that.

Two days later, Grace and I were back in the silent room, working on our group project. Jaimie had insisted we meet after school on account of the fact that we sucked at our parts. I was actually quite grateful to Jaimie. Both Blake and Grace had been no shows at school the day before. I'd assumed Grace was either too upset or hadn't been able to cover up the bruise Blake had left on her face. As for Blake, I imagined he was sleeping off his binge somewhere.

"You forgot this," I said, handing Grace back her notebook. Jaimie was trying to get everyone to focus, but Jimmy was chatting up the other girls, trying to convince any one of them to go out with him.

"Don't worry," I quickly added when I saw the worry on her face. "I couldn't read it."

Grace pressed her lips together, her worried expression changing over to something else I couldn't figure out. "Yeah, right," she said in that familiar snarky tone I was starting to grow used to. Why didn't she use her piss-poor attitude on Blake?

"No. Honest," I said, looking at her head on now. Not only did I want her to trust me, but I was trying to figure out how she'd gone and covered up the bruise on her left cheek so well. Good makeup and a lot of practice, I supposed, but now that I knew the truth about their relationship, no amount of makeup could hide what I'd seen the other night.

Grace looked at me a little weird, like she didn't really believe me. There was no point in arguing. Even if I did think it would help my cause to convince her, Jaimie was tired of Jimmy using up her precious time to try to get himself laid. "Come on, people!" she yelled. "We only have a week to memorize our lines, and I'll be damned if I'm gonna get a C on this project because of all of you."

Trying to get her to trust me, I urged Grace on in my own little way by saying, "You got Jimbo good today." Earlier that afternoon Mr. Reynolds had announced that the group would be given a collective grade, causing Jaimie to completely lose it.

Jimmy had told Jaimie to chill out.

Everyone had laughed. Everyone except Grace. "Leave her alone, Jimmy," Grace had said, before Mr. Reynolds told us to all to be quiet.

Instead of smiling, she glared at me. Sheesh. No one ever said playing by your own set of rules would be easy. At the very least, it was one small step toward getting Grace to stand up for herself.

Trying to get us all back on track, Jaimie directed each person on what they should do and when they should do it.

As each person took turns delivering their lines, I couldn't keep my mind focused. I thought about that night Grace had just cowered at Blake's hand. Why hadn't she screamed? Or run away? It confused me how she could be a total ball-yanker when it came to Jimmy and me, but a pussy cat with Blake.

Jaimie was giving us some hints on how to put more feeling into our lines when my eyes drifted up from the page. Normally, I didn't notice things like this, but from where I was, I could see the curve of Grace's left ear and the tiny gold stud pressed into the lobe. The stud reminded me of the stars I'd seen two nights before. Grace's nose twitched as if she was fighting off a sneeze. When she thought no one was looking, her face relaxed into an expression that made her look just like the girl in the photo albums.

"Cooper!" Jaimie's screechy voice pulled me out of my thoughts.

"Huh? Oh," I said, realizing it was my turn to read. I'd completely lost my place.

The girl who was playing Regan (Lana, was it?) was sitting next to me. "Here," she said. She leaned over my book and turned to the page with the scene we were on. As she did this, she pressed her chest into my arm. I saw Jimmy staring at me, a deep frown on his face.

"There you go," she said to me.

"Uh, thanks."

"Anytime."

Old habits are hard to kick. I found my eyes irresistibly drawn to Lana's cleavage.

Just like Mr. Reynolds, Jaimie cleared her throat. Before reading, I glanced over at Grace. Her face was buried in her book, but it was pink, almost blotchy. What was her issue?

For the first time since I'd sat next to her on the bleachers, my heart tripped over itself. Was that jealousy

Grace was trying to hide behind the pages of her book?

My heart wasn't the only thing tripping over itself. My tongue stumbled over the words. Instead of reciting them, I sounded like I was weed-whacking them to death. "Um . . . howl, howl, howl. Um, you are . . . um, men of stones."

"OMG!" Jaimie looked at me like I was a moron. "You call that acting? If we're lucky, Mr. Reynolds will give us a C. Maybe."

"What's the matter with a C?" Jimmy asked.

Jaimie ran her hand through her hair and shook her head. She looked like she was about to cry.

"If you read it like you mean it and don't keep saying "um," then maybe it wouldn't sound so bad," Grace said to me. The sharpness to her tone didn't seem to be about the play, but at least she was talking to me again.

If debating was the only way to get her to talk to me, I took the bait. "Well, if I knew what the heck the words meant, maybe I would read it the way you want me to."

Grace sighed like I was some little kid. "For one thing, *King Lear* is a tragedy."

Apparently, in this world, football buddies trumped football buddies' girlfriends. Jimmy came to my defense. "If you ask me, the real tragedy is that we have to read this crap."

Afraid I was going to lose her attention again, I ignored Jimmy's crack. "So what if *King Lear* is a tragedy? Why should that matter?"

"It matters a lot," Grace explained. "Shakespeare created tragedies and set up really bad situations for his characters. He didn't do this so they could just find happily-ever-after endings."

"Sounds depressing," Lana said. "I like stories with happy endings, don't you?" Lana smiled at me. When she said this, she sat forward. Fighting my own basic instincts, I leaned away.

"So why did he write his stories that way?" I asked.

"Shakespeare wanted the people who came to his plays to ask themselves questions." Grace was looking straight at me as she spoke.

"I thought people back then went to plays for the same reason we go to movies," Jimmy said. "Going to a play sounds more like going to school."

Jaimie rolled her eyes.

I was sure that Grace was thinking she was only wasting her breath. With the exception of Jaimie, I guess we looked like a bunch of idiots to her. But what about those questions? Did she have those questions, too?

Grace shut up.

Jaimie whipped out her SparkNotes. She started talking about themes and symbolism. I tried to listen for any clues as to what might be going through Grace's head. But Lucy hadn't said there'd be a test to prove I'd learned anything. So, after a while, my brain switched off.

Lana made another attempt to flirt with me. In another lifetime, I would have rolled myself all up in her like a dog in a big pile of dung, but I wasn't in the mood.

The announcements came over the loudspeaker that the late buses were there, and everyone got up to go.

Since we had an assignment in common, I thought about asking Grace if she wanted to come over and run through some lines together. As soon as I got up from my chair, there was Lana, all pressed up against me, yammering on about a fundraiser the cheerleaders were having.

"Will you come?" she asked. Her cleavage, which she brushed up against my chest, also seemed to have a vested interest in my going.

"I'd like to, but I can't," I said.

Lana looked like a little kid who had just been told her dog died.

"Sorry," I said, trying to move around Lana's puppies. The girl was like gum. By the time I could unstick myself, Grace was nowhere to be found.

CHAPTER 12

△

The next day was Saturday. With no school, there was little chance of running into Grace unless I made one. I decided I'd take one of the bikes from the garage and ride over to her house. Hopefully, Blake wouldn't be lurking around. I'd act casual and, if Grace gave me a chance, I would try to explain about how I was Cooper, but not the Cooper she thought I was. Of course, I wasn't going to tell her the truth. That would really freak her out. But maybe if I got all sentimental with her and showed her I was the Cooper she remembered, the one from the photo albums, then she would see we could be friends again.

As I thought more about my plan, I fantasized about what it might be like to be more than friends with Grace. From those old pictures, and the way I caught Grace looking at me from time to time, I had a feeling there might have once been more. For now, though, I had to convince Grace not to slam the door in my face.

I was just about to head out the door when I stopped myself. Last night, after I'd finally figured out how to find the house again, Mom and Dad had been kind of worried.

"Your mother almost had me on the phone with the police, Cooper," Dad had said. I'd only half believed the Wandermans would call out the National Guard, but they really were those types of people.

So today, just so they could relax, I went to find Mom to let her know I was going out. She was standing at the counter working on a Sudoku puzzle. A big basket of unfolded laundry was sitting in a plastic tub on the table next to her. "This puzzle is driving me crazy," she said.

I had to smile. She'd worked on that puzzle all day yesterday. In between cooking and making telephone calls for her job, she'd go back to it and plug in a different combination. I watched her frown, than erase a whole line. I knew how she felt.

"I'm going out for a bike ride," I said.

"Hmmm?" she said, studying the squares. "Oh! Okay. Hey, could you do me a favor?"

She stuck the pencil she was using between the pages of her book and went to the fridge. As she did, I looked around the kitchen again. The lace curtains, the bunch of bananas sitting in the fruit bowl turning ripe, the leftover pie left sitting out from last night's dinner . . . to someone else, these details would go unnoticed. To me, they were a sign that a family lived here, and somehow, in a matter of a few short days, I'd melted right into the routine. Weird.

I warned myself not to get too attached. Like Mom's Sudoku puzzle, Lucy could rub me out and replace me with someone else.

"Here." Mom handed me a brown paper bag. It was the same kind of bag she packed my lunch in, only this one had Ryan's name printed on it. "Can you take this down to your brother at work? He forgot it."

To me it didn't make sense to bring lunch to someone who worked at a deli, but I took the bag. "Sure. No problem."

Mom went back to her Sudoku and I headed out. The last thing she said to me before I walked out the door was, "And don't eat your brother's dessert!"

By the time I rounded the street where Grace lived, I

was already downing a second mini powdered donut. At least I thought it was Grace's street. As I pedaled, I looked for the house, but none matched up with the house I had in my memory. Maybe I'd taken a wrong turn.

I rode the full length of the road. I could have sworn it was where Grace lived. My skin crawled when I saw the familiar arc of trees a few houses down from where I was standing. I rode my bike closer, looking for the path I had taken two nights before, but there was no noticeable gap in the trees.

I heard a fragment of a chime in the not too far-off distance. "Not this time, Lucy," I said to myself, thinking Lucy was messing with me again. The woman really needed to get a hobby.

A few people were out working on their lawns. A couple of kids ran up and down the sidewalks, chasing each other. In the daylight, without Blake around to run me down, the street seemed like a nice place to live. I rode up and down the street one more time, but I couldn't pinpoint which house it was.

I approached one of the little kids and said, "Hey! Do you know where Grace Sanders lives?"

The kid shook his head and went back to his game.

"Can I help you?" One of the men who'd been trimming some bushes outside his house called over. I guess, around there, someone like me might have earned a suspicious look or two. Then I remembered, at least on the surface, I wasn't that punk kid anymore. If anything, I looked like a walking ad for the Ivy League with my clean cut hair and neat shirt – a shirt I'd pulled out from the button-down collection in the other Cooper Wanderman's closet.

"Do you know where the Sanders live?" I asked the man.

The man shook his head. "Nobody by that name lives on Fairview." And as if he wanted to make sure there was no question about it, he added, "And I should know. I'm in charge of the neighborhood watch."

Point taken. I waved good-bye to the guy and pedaled off.

For another hour, I rode up and down every street in the area. Every street was a carbon copy of the next one. To make matters worse, they all dead-ended at the woods and the now familiar *No Trespassing* sign. Whoever planned these neighborhoods had used the woods as a kind of hub with the streets jutting out like spokes. It might not have been a bad plan if the woods weren't so creepy. Then again, not everyone had a She-Devil messing with them.

The oily smell drifting from Ryan's lunch bag told me it was time to get moving. Reluctantly, I gave up my search.

"It's about time," Ryan said, when I showed up. "I'm starved." There was a wooden bench outside the deli. I hung out with Ryan while he took his lunch break.

"Want half?" Ryan said, offering me his sandwich.

I shook my head. "Are you sure you want to eat that?" I said. "Why don't you just get something from inside?"

"Don't you know, Boomer, that there are no free lunches in life?" Ryan said.

I'd heard the expression before, from one of the long line of social workers who'd managed my case for more years than I could remember. I'd never really understood what she'd meant by it.

"So your boss doesn't give you free lunch. So what? It's better than eating a soggy tuna sandwich, isn't it?"

Ryan laughed. "I'm not talking about literal free lunches."

"Oh," I said. I hated when people did that, held back on what they really wanted to say just so they could make the other person feel stupid.

"What I mean is, nobody just goes around handing out free opportunities," he said.

I slung my arms across my chest and shrugged like I knew exactly what he meant.

Ryan sucked on the straw of his juice box. I guessed what Ryan was talking about was his scholarship being taken away. If I was him, I would have been pretty worked up over it. Instead he just sat there like an old banana peel thrown on the street, ready to be stepped on.

Ryan looked in the bag to see what else Mom had packed. Instead of getting mad that I'd eaten his dessert, he said nothing, which made me feel a little guilty, which in turn made me even more disgusted that he didn't defend himself.

I wanted to ask Ryan about Grace, but I knew it was a touchy subject. I decided to approach it in a different way.

"Any cute chicks around here?" I asked, scanning the street corner where the deli sat.

"Only if you count Mrs. Milford, who comes down every day and orders exactly three slices of bologna," he laughed. "Why, you got your eye on anyone?"

Trying to sound cool and steering away from the topic of Grace, I said, "Well, there is this one girl, Lana, in my English class. She's pretty hot."

Ryan sucked the last bit of juice out of the box making a *squitch*, *squitch* sound. "That's good. Just keep it casual. The last time you lost your head over a girl . . ." Ryan hesitated like he didn't know if he should finish.

"What?" I said.

"Nothing. It's just when you and Grace were together, it was cute in the beginning when the two of you talked back and forth in that code you made up. But afterwards . . ." Ryan stopped again like he was afraid of taking me back to that time. But that's exactly what I needed, to be taken back so I could figure out what I was dealing with.

"What secret code?" I said, forgetting I was supposed to know this stuff.

"You're not serious, Boomer. You're honestly telling me you don't remember?" Ryan stared at me.

I tried to keep my cool. "Sure, it's just that it was a long time ago. History." I was trying to come off casual while still getting him to talk.

"Yeah. History," Ryan repeated. I tried to stay expressionless. It must have been convincing, because Ryan opened up. "You must have found out about it online. "Ubbi Dubbi," it was called."

"That's right! Ubbi Dubbi." I nodded like I was honestly remembering.

"Mom said it came from some old TV show for kids that was around when she was growing up." Ryan rolled his eyes. "You wanted all of us to speak it. You drove us crazy with it."

He suddenly got up. "Yeah, well. I gotta get back to work." But the way he rubbed his hand through his hair and looked down at the cracks in the sidewalk, I could tell there was a lot more he could have said if he'd wanted to.

"Thanks for bringing my lunch." Ryan crumpled up his lunch bag and shot a three-pointer into the trash can.

I was drenched in sweat by the time I got home.

"Cooper?" Mom called out from the kitchen. But this time I was in too big a rush to stop.

I ran upstairs, stopping first to grab the pad of paper I'd left on my desk. Dad's office, which was a small room just off their bedroom, had a computer in it. Luckily, he'd left the computer on before he'd gone out to play golf so I didn't need a password to get in.

I got to the search bar and typed in "Ubi Dubi language." Google's response was *Did you mean Ubbi Dubbi?*

I clicked on that, and holy crap! Ryan wasn't kidding when he'd said Ubbi Dubbi actually existed. According to the article I read, Ubbi Dubbi was a language game, sort of like Pig Latin or something else I'd never heard of called Double Dutch. There were even instructions showing how to take a regular word and turn it into Ubbi Dubbi. It was actually really easy. All you had to do was put the letters ub or ubi in front of each vowel in each syllable of the word. There was an example that showed how hubi translated into hi.

Now that I saw it, I couldn't believe how easy it was to follow the pattern. This was how Grace and I used to talk to each other? I thought of Grace's notebook. If she still remembered the code, did that mean she still thought of when she and I were friends? I supposed it was kind of a stretch to think of it this way. But, if she really didn't like me, wouldn't she want to forget all about everything we'd ever done before? The way I was holding onto this flimsy idea made me realize how into this girl I really was.

The site had a translator where you could put in an English word and it would be translated into Ubbi Dubbi. There was also a way to do it in the opposite direction. I took the pad of paper where I'd written some of what I'd found in Grace's notebook and plugged what looked to be the first sentence into the translator.

Ubevuben thubough Ubim nubot dubead Ubi mubight ubias wubiell bubie. Even though I'm not dead, I might as well be.

The meaning of the words startled me. I knew it was bad between Blake and Grace, but this proved how really bad it was. Then I remembered I'd pulled this sentence from an entry Grace had written in her notebook years ago. Were the two of them even dating back then? Something didn't make sense.

There was another sentence. I didn't need to plug this one into the translator to understand it though. *This promise is killing me.*

What promise was Grace talking about?

Even though Ryan had warned me against it, I couldn't just sit by doing nothing. Using the computer again, I looked up a phone number. Then I reached for the phone on Dad's desk.

"I was just talking about you, man," Blake said when he answered the phone.

At first I thought it was weird that he'd known it was me. Then I remembered caller I.D.

Trying to keep my anger in check the best way I knew how, I acted casual and said, "Yeah? What about?"

"I'm having a party tonight. Come by."

Perfect. I gave Blake a quick yes to the invite and then made some excuse that I had to go help my father mow the lawn. Before hanging up the phone, I thought I heard someone laughing on the other end. I pressed the phone quick to my ear, but Blake had already hung up.

Strange. I would have expected a much deeper laugh from someone Blake's size.

Until Mom called me down for dinner, I sat in Dad's chair. There was a lighter on his desk. I picked it up and flicked it again and again, looking into the flame. If Lucy had sent me back down here to escape Hell, then why did I have the feeling that somehow I was walking straight into the flames?

CHAPTER 13

When I got to Blake's, the place was a mad house. Not only was the entire football team there, but so were the cheerleaders, along with a whole slew of party crashers who'd probably heard about it online.

Someone I didn't recognize answered the door. The minute I walked in the house, the stench of beer stung my nose. Lucy's makeover was having some unexpected effects on me because the first question that came to mind was where were Blake's parents?

The music was loud and the furniture had been shoved against the walls allowing for every last inch of space to be filled by writhing teenage bodies keeping time with the thudding music.

Over the loud bass beat, I heard someone yell my name. "Coop!" When I turned around, there was Jimmy. He was carrying three beers and he offered me one. Normally, I would have grabbed all three, but tonight I waved the offer off, knowing I would need a clear head and fast feet when I confronted Blake.

Jimmy's eyes were bloodshot. The kid was totally plastered, but that didn't stop him from snapping back the tab on another beer.

"Have you seen Blake?" I yelled.

Jimmy let out a ridiculously long burp then pointed in the direction of the kitchen.

Pushing through a parade of more bodies, I found my way to there. A group of girls hung out by the chips, and some guy who played tight end had a girl pinned against the refrigerator. She looked kind of young and was giggling nervously.

"Hey, man. You seen Blake?" I asked him. The guy turned, giving the girl a chance to wiggle free from his clutches.

The guy, who was clearly drunk, looked annoyed. That was when another girl stepped up and smiled. "Aren't you going to say hi?" she asked. From the smell of her breath and her red glassy eyes, she'd knocked back a few too many too.

Had it not been for the two wiggling puppies squirming to get out of the girl's top, I would not have remembered her. "Oh, Lana! Hey!"

"Wanna dance? Or do something else?" Lana teased, though it was obviously a legitimate offer on her part.

The old me would have jumped on an offer like that, but when I looked at Lana, her drunken grin sickened me.

"No thanks," I said.

Lana's posse of girlfriends giggled behind her, and Lana looked as if she was about to cry.

On impulse, I leaned forward and whispered in Lana's ear so no one else could hear. "Go home, Lana," I said. Then I gave her a soft peck on the cheek.

As I was leaving the kitchen, I heard Lana's friends laugh and swoon.

I found Blake outside in the hot tub. He was in there with three girls who looked like they'd just graduated seventh grade.

Blake was pouring a can of beer into the churning water, daring the girls to drink it, when he saw me. "Coopman!"

The hot tub was tucked away in a corner on the patio.

The patio was filled with people. Taking a quick glance around, I didn't see the pink-haired girl I was looking for.

"Don't bother looking for her, Coop," Blake said. "She's not here."

I looked back at Blake. He was getting out of the hot tub, drying himself off with a towel. There was no denying he was one of the biggest guys I'd ever seen, bigger than the Rasta-albino and a heck of a lot more intimidating.

Blake moved in, filling up the space meant for both of us. Only this time, instead of getting me in a headlock, Blake got me in a kind of bear hug. His actions might have looked chummy to the seventh grade graduates who were laughing and saying, "Aren't they cute!" But by the way he was squeezing me, I wondered if it was possible to die twice.

"Aw, come on, Coop. Don't deny it. I know you like Grace. But remember friends don't hit on other friends' chicks."

This time when I wiggled my way out of Blake's hold, I had the feeling it had less to do with me and more to do with him not wanting to make too much of a scene. Already, kids were flooding the deck, craning their necks over each other to see what was going on.

I, for one, was happy for the audience. When I'd gotten some air back in my lungs, I said, "I'm not hitting on Grace. I'm just here to tell you to stop treating her the way you do."

Blake looked like he'd just eaten some of Mom's tuna. I could tell I'd crossed a line I could never walk back over again. Something in his eyes changed. His pupils flicked red, and a sick feeling hit me in the gut. I was reminded of what I'd seen in the woods.

Blake looked away. "If you know what's good for you, Coopman, you'll leave," he said. His eyes weren't red anymore, but the anger in his face was still there.

Confused by what I thought I'd just seen, I stepped back. The crowd parted, and somehow I was back on the street not knowing how I'd gotten there.

I don't know how long I stood there, but, like the day I'd set that fire, I was itchy to do something, anything. Pulling out my cell phone, I dialed Grace's number. The call went straight to her all-too-familiar voice mail, but that time when I went to add another message, her mailbox was full. Where could she be?

I looked up at the sky, which was completely cloudless. If Lucy wanted me to help Grace, it was as good a time as any to give me a clue about what my next step should be.

Something tugged at me, and though it was the last thing I wanted to do, I headed for the woods.

Like all the other streets in town, I just had to follow Blake's street to the end. There, posted on the edge where the grass met the asphalt, sat the *No Trespassing* sign. If I'd had any sense, I would have heeded the advice. Luckily, Lucy's makeover hadn't included a dose of practicality.

At first I couldn't find the opening that led into the woods. I searched along the trees and bushes and must have passed the spot at least five times before I finally found the entrance. Just like the first time I'd walked along the pine-needle strewn woodland floor, I got the sense I wasn't supposed to be there. Keeping in mind that it was the only chance I had to talk to Lucy, I pushed forward.

As the trees above me thinned out, the clouds rolled in, and it became more difficult to find my way. I hoped that wasn't Lucy's way of telling me she wasn't in the mood to talk. Well, tough. I was tired of being in the dark, both literally and figuratively. For the rest of the way, I had to use my hands and feet, making sure I didn't get smacked in the head with a branch.

When I finally got to the clearing, the lighting was only a tiny bit better.

"Lucy!" I shouted into the darkness. "I know you can hear me!"

My heart pounded in my chest. I hated Lucy for keeping me waiting. She knew how I felt about the dark.

The breeze churned up, chasing the clouds across the sky. If I'd had half a brain I would have gotten out of there. A cracking sound, like someone stepping on a branch, shot me to attention. I turned around, but there was no sign of the beady-eyed monster or Lucy. I relaxed my stance for only a moment, but it was long enough for a pair of icy hands to sneak up from behind me and fling me across the clearing.

My body convulsed from the force of a dozen lightning bolts. Lucky for me, I landed in a pile of old tires that absorbed some of the impact. I willed my muscles to get me back on my feet and got ready to lunge at my attacker. There was no sign of anyone, or anything, for that matter.

It made no sense to spur my attacker on, but I was beyond all reason. If I couldn't defend Grace against Blake, then at least I could defend myself. "Come on out, you son-of-a-bitch!" I yelled.

This time when the icy hands cupped themselves around my neck, they maintained the pressure against my windpipe. Gasping for breath, I flung out my hands. I put up a good fight, but the grasp was so tight, all I could manage was to flail around like a crab in a net.

"You!" I said, but the word didn't actually leave my mouth. There wasn't enough air in my lungs to push it out.

Without oxygen, my body started going numb and so did my mind. As the world caved in around me, my last thought was of Grace.

Just as it had happened before, a soft halo of light engulfed me, the edges of which began to blur, and everything went white. I headed out, way, way out into a part of the outfield that most people never even knew existed. I was just about out of the stadium when someone grabbed me. There was a shriek, like someone was getting kicked hard in the shins. Then I was dragged back to home plate.

Maybe every time you died, it was different. Just because I'd done it once didn't mean there weren't variations on the scenario.

Then a voice penetrated the darkness. "Come on!" it urged.

I followed.

My head was still spinning, and I wasn't quite sure whether I was actually dead or alive. When I looked up and realized the voice belonged to Grace, dead or alive suddenly didn't matter. All that mattered was that she was there.

CHAPTER 14

△

A cloud was calling my name. I knew it was a cloud because it sounded floaty and soft. Rather than in words, the cloud spoke to me in whispery tones.

"Cooper?"

Since when did clouds call you by name?

"Cooper, it's me."

For a cloud, it sure was persistent. And it smelled good; I had to give it that.

It brushed itself against my arm, causing my own barometric pressure to go up.

"Cooper!"

Blinking, I looked up. The first thing I saw was the poster taped to the ceiling. What were the Jonas Brothers doing in the afterlife?

There was a subtle shift in the room. When I tried to turn my head, it felt like someone had replaced my brains with ball bearings.

"Cooper, wake up! It's me. Grace." The cloud wasn't a cloud at all, but in my opinion, she was still the bomb. Grace was leaning over me. Not only was she leaning over me, but she was lying down on the bed next to me. How I'd gotten on the bed, I had no clue. Though I sure wasn't complaining.

"How many fingers am I holding up?" Grace raised her

hand.

"Two," I answered quickly. I figured the sooner I answered her question, the sooner she'd go back to rubbing my arm with those two fingers. With very little space between us, I was acutely aware of the subtle heat lifting off of Grace's body. It reminded me of a hot day when the heat drifts up in waves off the asphalt. Only, it was a million times sexier.

"How do you feel?"

Not wanting to ruin the moment with something as minor as brain damage, I said, "Fine."

Grace sat up. She looked away from me and bit her lip. It was only a split second, but I already missed her.

Raising myself up to meet her proved to be a bad move. The Jonas Brothers started busting out in some kind of wavery break dance, and I felt like I was on the brink of puking.

Grace placed her hands gently behind my head and eased me back onto the bed. Then she sidled up close to me again. Okay, so if having permanent head spins was the sacrifice I had to make to get Grace to lie down next to me, then so be it.

"I'm really sorry, Cooper," Grace said. Her voice sounded muffled. At first I thought it was the ball bearings getting in the way between her lips and my ears. Then I realized Grace was crying.

Unlike my brain, my arms and hands still worked. I reached around Grace and pulled her close. Unfortunately, that only increased her sobs.

Grace leaned up on her elbow and wiped her face with the back of her hand. Her mouth was within kissing range.

"What are you sorry about?" I said.

"You mean you don't remember what happened? At all?"

With my free hand, I rubbed the side of my head. I felt

a lump the size of a golf ball where my head had come into contact with the tires. *So much for a soft landing*, I thought. "I remember going into the woods. There was this . . . thing." I wasn't really sure what to call whatever had clamped its cold hands around my neck, nearly squishing the life right out of me.

As I ran through these facts in my mind, more and more details from the night got clearer. "Before that, I went over to Blake's. I told him to stop being such a creep to you."

"You shouldn't have done that, Cooper," she said.

I couldn't believe what I was hearing. I was there, doing what Lucy wanted me to do. No, nix that. I was doing what I wanted to do, and Grace was still refusing my help?

"But how can you just let Blake treat you that way?" I said.

Unlike with Blake, Grace had no problem detaching herself from me. She got up and started pacing the room. My head hurt less, so I chanced it. I eased myself up to a sitting position. That time I was more successful and didn't topple over.

"So what was that thing and how did you save me?" I said.

"I don't know what you're talking about, Cooper," Grace said. "You were at Blake's and you had too much to drink, so I brought you back here to my house. That's all I know."

While a lot of the night before was still fuzzy, there was one thing I was clear about. "You were there, Grace. In the forest," I said. "I don't know how you did it, but you managed to get both of us out before something really bad happened."

Just for good measure, to show her I wasn't as dumb as she thought, I said, "And by the way, Grace. You may think you're a good liar, but, if you ask me, you can't lie to save your life."

"Or yours," Grace mumbled.

"What did you just say?"

Grace's face blazed red and she continued to insist that what I remembered was just a result of too much beer. "You don't know what you're talking about, Cooper. I've seen you like this before. You drink too much and then you have all sorts of nightmares. I told Blake you're a lightweight, that you can't handle your booze like he can."

Even if Grace didn't look like a caged tiger, walking her room from end to end as she said all that, I wasn't buying it.

"I know what I saw, Grace. And what I saw was you going neck-to-neck with that creature and saving my butt in the process. You can't deny it, so stop trying."

Grace looked down at the small dish of dried flower petals sitting on her dresser. Putting her hand in the dish, she crumbled the petals until they were nothing more than a fine powder.

"Come on, Grace. Don't you think you owe it to me to tell me what's going on here? If you didn't want to tell me, then why did you bring me here of all places?"

Grace sighed. "I brought you here because this is the only safe place for you. When I made my promise, this room was my only condition."

The situation was a lot worse than I thought. "You had to make Blake promise to stay away from here?" I said.

Grace looked at me. In her eyes I saw something I didn't quite understand. "You don't remember anything, do you?" she said.

Now, I understood what I was seeing. Grace was feeling sorry, not for herself, but for me.

"Yeah, I remember. I just told you what I saw in the woods, didn't I?" Even to my own ears, I could hear how defensive I sounded.

Grace shook her head. "I'm not talking about what happened at Blake's or the woods," she said. "I'm talking about what happened to us two years ago."

That would have been as good a time as any for Lucy to text me a cheat sheet. Of course, Lucy was never one to make these things easy.

My head was still swimming, and I was too tired of lying. "No, I can't remember," I admitted.

The minute the truth touched my lips I was sure Grace would go back to treating me like a guy with a really bad hangover. Instead, the truth had the opposite effect, and like one of my Bible-thumping caseworkers had once said, truth begets truth.

"Okay, Cooper," Grace said. "You win."

Grace sat on the edge of the bed so that we were sitting side by side. Her proximity was not something I took lightly, and by the way she was twining and untwining her fingers, I could tell it wasn't something Grace took for granted, either. She studied my face the way some people study a map, judging what direction to head in next.

"Look at me, Cooper," she said. And when I did it was like I'd discovered my own true north.

The storm clouds that had been covering up the light in Grace's eyes now parted, and a beam of light pulled me close. "Oh!" I said and looked away. For a moment, I thought I'd recognized something. A past. My past.

I was still trying to shake away the odd feeling when Grace put her hand on my face and said, "Look at me, Cooper." She forced me to look in her eyes. Then we kissed. She pressed her lips hard against mine, and the memory I'd only caught a glimpse of bloomed in my mind's eye as fully as a movie.

Only it was no movie. Every scene and every sensation ripped through my body. The things I was seeing and feeling were pieces of me, pieces of a life.

While I fought against the pictures flooding my mind, Grace fought to keep her lips glued to mine. She needed me

109

to see those things.

One of the memories was warm and sunny. I recognized where I was immediately. Instead of old tires and litter, small purple flowers covered the woodland floor. Grace and I were side by side on a blanket. A small stone dug into my hip bone, but I was too busy looking at her to care. She was beautiful. A little younger and with honey-colored hair. A strand fell from Grace's pony tail. It took all the courage I had to push it behind her ear. My gut told me that was the small crack Lucifer had been waiting for.

He slipped right through, and as the memory sharpened, my instinct was to pull away. Grace pushed her lips against me, willing me not to let go.

Back in the memory, a shivery cloud fell over our picnic. The wind howled and the world ripped apart. Grace was screaming, but instead of helping her, all I could do was flail around. Again, the breath had been crushed right out of me. I started slipping into a black hole. Further and further I dropped, but all I cared about was Grace.

When I opened my eyes, I was shaking. Beads of sweat collected on my forehead.

"I died," I choked. The sensation of falling down that black tunnel was still so real that I couldn't calm my body down from shuddering. That black void hadn't been anything like the peaceful warmth I'd felt the first time around.

"It's okay, Cooper." Grace was rubbing my back and talking quietly, doing anything she could to keep me from freaking out. Afraid of a repeat performance, I avoided looking into her eyes.

"I don't blame you if you don't want to look at me, but I promise that's it," Grace said. "It won't happen again. Lucifer told me if I ever did choose to show you what happened on that day, I'd only have one chance and that was it."

"Lucifer? So, you're on a first name basis with the guy?" I said. I realized the moment I said it how stupid it was coming from me of all people.

Grace looked at her hands. It wasn't my intention to make her feel guilty, only I was still trying to wrap my mind around what I'd just seen.

"I'm sorry," I said. "It's just that I'm not getting it. And I don't remember any of it."

"That's exactly how he wants you to feel," Grace said. ""Lucifer is the one who took you away. And that's who tried to kill you again last night."

The look of shock on my face must have given Grace the impression that I didn't believe her. She pulled back from me a bit. "You think I'm crazy, don't you?"

"Of all the things going through my mind right now," I told her, "you being crazy is not even close to making the list."

That seemed to relax her, for once again she sidled up to me. Greedily, I looped my arms around her and planted my nose in her hair. As Grace recounted the rest of what had happened that day, I continued to breathe her in. Her sweet scent helped to ground me, to come to grips with the story of our life – our real life – together.

"As much as I've tried to pinpoint it, that day wasn't any different from any other day," Grace explained. "We loved going to the woods. When we were little, we used to play manhunt. But as we got older, we weren't much interested in games. We would talk. I'd bore you for hours with all the details of my parents' divorce, but you would listen. You were always such a good listener, Cooper."

That detail about myself surprised me.

"We were as close as any two people could be. Your mom used to say we were like two peas in a pod. And Ryan used to tease us that we were going to get married someday. We even had our own secret code."

"Ubbi Dubbi," I said.

"Yeah," she smiled. "It sounds really stupid now, I guess. But you liked the idea of having our own secret language."

I thought about Grace's notebook. When I'd first seen it, I'd only thought she was weird for writing like that. But now I saw that the notebook was Grace's only safe way of expressing her feelings.

"That day on the blanket," Grace continued, "that was the first day you'd ever told me you loved me. Then you kissed me."

Just like the sensation of Grace's recent kiss, the kiss from that day was still so vivid. How had I ever been able to forget it?

"Our kiss is what brought him?" I asked.

Grace nodded. "We had no way of knowing how jealous Lucifer was. He hates human love, Cooper. It threatens him, I think. And we were so young, and we already knew we wanted to be together. Some people, maybe most people, never find what we had. Our kind of love threatens Lucifer because he's afraid that we could give other people hope. Hope is the last thing he wants to encourage."

Grace took a moment. The next part was clearly harder for her to say. I traced my thumb along the inside of her arm and waited patiently.

"When you were close to dying, he forced me to watch," she said. "Just when I was sure you couldn't hang on any longer, he whispered in my ear. He told me if I took another path, if I rejected you and loved him instead, he would spare you."

"So you made a deal with him and he let me go? But what about you?" Before I'd only been worried about one monster, but Lucifer made Blake look like a pussycat in comparison.

Grace's voice steadied. "I made the right choice. I've

never regretted it, Cooper. It is what it is, and we have to accept it. I'm just happy you remember me again."

My mind was reeling. The anger I felt was enough to burn down an entire city. And again, where was Lucy in all of this?

"This doesn't make sense. I had this whole other life. I was in foster homes. Oh, my God, Grace! I even burned down a school. And now you're saying that wasn't ever me?"

"I know it's difficult for you to understand," she said.

Shaking my head, I was starting to wonder if the lump on the back of my head was more serious than I had previously thought.

"Are you telling me none of that was real? That my body has been here this whole time playing football and having dinner with my family every night?"

"A part of you has been doing those things, yes. But a part of you was . . . elsewhere."

As she tried to explain it to me, it made less and less sense each time. Finally, she got up and walked over to her desk. From the top drawer, Grace took a deck of playing cards.

"See these cards?" she asked, shuffling the deck.

I looked at the cards sullenly. This was hardly the moment for her to be showing me a magic trick. Reluctantly, I nodded.

Grace placed the whole deck on the palm of her hand. "Like this, you would count the cards as one deck, right? But then when you cut the deck in two, it becomes your life, Cooper. When the Devil took you away from me, he split your life into two parts. The part of you that didn't remember me stayed here. But this part . . ." Grace cut the deck and handed me the other half.

She tapped the cards sitting in my hand. "This part went somewhere else for a while. But it looks like now you're back," she said, reuniting both smaller decks into one.

Lucifer's methods put Hugh Everett's theories about parallel universes to shame. "But now you remember me again. I don't know how it happened. But you do."

Lucy happened, I thought to myself. Though I wasn't quite ready to explain that to Grace. All I wanted to do was hold her, which is what I did. We fell back on her bed. The heaviness in my head lifted and a new, happy feeling replaced the weight. The happiness was not without its burden, however.

"So now that I remember, the deal's off?" I told Grace. This would go not only for Grace's deal with Lucifer, but my deal with Lucy, too. The two of them could get on the next rocket straight for Hell.

Grace pulled herself into me as far as she could. "It doesn't work that way, Cooper."

After that I didn't say anything, not because I wanted to avoid arguing with her, but because I was afraid she was right.

CHAPTER 15

△

Later, when I walked into the house, everything was eerily quiet. In the kitchen, the soft *thunk, thunk, thunk* of the drippy faucet echoed my thoughts. Now that I knew what had really happened, I was afraid Lucifer would find a way to ruin my life again.

It wasn't only me that was worried. Before I'd left her house, Grace had circled her arms around my waist.

"He's more powerful than you know, Cooper," she'd said. She was holding onto me for dear life. The only problem was it was still my life Grace was worried about. Not her own.

In between kissing, I'd hoped to convince her there was a way out. I'd even told her about Lucy. But Grace was even more stubborn than I was.

"The time we've had together is a gift," she'd said. "We don't know what Lucifer will do. He might just let this slide, but you can't push this any further, Cooper."

From all our talking, it was finally sinking in how helpless we really were. I'd told Grace about how I'd been looking for her house and had gotten lost in the process.

She wasn't surprised. "That's part of what Lucifer does. He turns a person's world upside down. Sometimes you really believe something is true, only to find out he's completely playing you. Sometimes I don't even know who my own parents are. I mean they do and say the same thing they always did, but still . . ."

Grace hadn't bothered finishing her thought. She was like a beautiful butterfly trying not to get knocked down by the wind.

At that point I recognized where the flutter in my chest was coming from. All those butterflies in my chest, trying to fly free? It had been my heart this whole time, trying to find Grace.

Before letting me go, Grace had said, "Promise me you won't take any more risks?"

In her mind, I was sure that on her list of risks for me, she'd written her own name. But if that was Grace's way of making me promise I would never see her again, there was just no way. Keeping promises was Grace's specialty. Not mine.

As I stared at the coffee pot, my mind was blank. I'd be damned twice to let Grace deal with this on her own.

The coffee pot, which Mom had pre-programmed the night before, sat ready, its glass carafe filled to the brim. It was Sunday, the only day everyone got to sleep in. I'd seen the effects coffee had on my father and how much he needed it. So why wasn't he sitting at the kitchen table, already downing his fourth cup? The sight of that full coffee pot made me edgy.

When Ryan walked into the kitchen, I had to stop myself from giving him a giant bear hug. Not only was I relieved to see him safe, but the more Grace and I talked the night before, the more I had remembered about my old life. Looking at Ryan in his Scooby Doo pajama bottoms, I could now recall how he'd taught me to ride a two-wheeler and how, even though I'd ridden over his toes more than a few times, he hadn't given up on me.

Strong as the impulse was to give my brother a hug, I

held back. Even more than before, it was important to keep my cool and pretend I was just the same old Cooper. Not revealing what I knew also extended to Blake.

"Blake is Lucifer's minion," Grace had explained. "Blake keeps an eye on me. If he sees you remembering or acting any differently, both our lives and the lives of our families will be in danger."

I worried about the night before and how, for the second time, Grace had rescued me. Grace said she would find a way to take care of it, but I was afraid it might mean another sacrifice on her part.

"Someone looks like they had a rockin' night." Ryan plucked a banana from the fruit bowl and slouched down in a chair.

I sat down next to him. "Yeah, right." Sitting this close to Ryan, I couldn't help but pick up a faint sugary-sweet smell about him. "What about you?" I said. "You smell like you've been rolling around in cupcake frosting. Who's the lucky girl?" It was nice to kid around like we were just two normal brothers.

Ryan chewed the last bit of banana. "Don't I wish," he said. "My friend Jack hooked me up with a guy who owns a bakery downtown. At night when the place is closed, I go in and scrape up all the glaze that's stuck to the floor."

I imagined Ryan spending his night breaking his back as he dug through a rock-hard mixture of dried up sugar and water. I started wondering. Was Ryan's bad luck in any way connected to what was going on with me and Grace?

"I get to take any leftover donuts home. See, I brought you a box." Ryan pointed in the direction of the microwave.

I hadn't noticed the box of donuts before. They looked a little deformed, but they hardly seemed like a sign of bad luck.

When I picked up the donut box, Ryan asked, "What's that?"

Stuck under the box was a note. Ryan grabbed it before I could get it.

"Shoot, Cooper!" he said. "Dad took Mom to the hospital last night."

I grabbed the note from his hand and read it. The note said very little, just that they'd gone to the hospital.

"I'm gonna call Dad," Ryan said.

As he called, a familiar cold feeling wrapped itself around my neck. I stood there watching Ryan and waiting for Dad to pick up on the other end.

Ryan put down the phone and frowned. "The call went straight to Dad's voice mail."

I was about to tell Ryan to try Mom's cell, but he was already starting on her number.

I held my breath. The kitchen was so quiet that I could hear Mom's voice on the other end of the line. My momentary relief disappeared when it turned out to be her voice mail. Ryan tried to leave a message, but her mailbox was full.

"That's weird," Ryan said. "Mom always clears out her mailbox for work."

But it wasn't weird. Not to me. Lucifer was showing some real lack of creativity. The tactics he was using to keep us from Mom were the same ones he'd used to keep me away from Grace.

Ryan sat down and looked at the note. "It's not like Dad to just leave us hanging this way. Remember the last time he and Mom left for their trip to Ireland? They said good-night to us the night before, but then woke us up at four-thirty in the morning just so they could say good-bye again."

"They wanted to make sure we knew where all the emergency numbers were," I said. Funny how I could remember this now. I also remembered the four-leaf clover charm they'd brought me back as a souvenir. I was happy that memories were coming back, but angry, too, that Lucifer had robbed me of so much.

"They must have been in a rush." Ryan looked like he was thinking of all of the possibilities, but there was no way his imagination was skipping around the way mine was.

I worried that Mom wasn't in the hospital, and it hadn't been Dad at all who'd written the note. I was afraid that Grace's predictions were starting to come true. The look on Ryan's face, and the quiet that now consumed the house, were overwhelming. Now I understood why I'd fallen so easily into Cooper Wanderman's sneakers. I *was* Cooper Wanderman. And this was my family. Aside from the memories of Ryan and my bike, it was Dad's stupid jokes and Mom's hugs that all started feeling like important pieces of a puzzle I'd never known I was trying to piece together. While I'd been ripped away from Grace, I'd also been taken away from my parents and Ryan. Not only was I desperate to hold onto Grace and my family, I wanted to take back everything Lucifer had ever stripped away from me.

"I think I hear the car," Ryan said. We both went to the door and looked out the window at the empty driveway. As much as Ryan pretended he had it pulled together better than me, his face, with the pinched lines around his mouth, revealed otherwise.

Like two little kids, we stood waiting at the door. A half hour passed and both Ryan and I tried Mom and Dad's cells for at least the twentieth time. When Dad's car finally turned into the driveway, both of us bolted outside.

Mom's face looked pale as Dad helped her out of the passenger-side seat.

"Hi, guys," Dad said. While his words sounded casual, I could tell by his face that it had been a rough night.

Mom managed a small smile, but I could tell she was in a lot of pain and concentrating hard on managing the few steps to the front door.

The minute Dad was done helping Mom settle herself

into bed, he came back down to the kitchen. Ryan and I had a million questions for him.

"What happened?"

"Is she in pain?"

"Why does she seem so out of it?"

"What did the doctors say?"

"Is she going to be alright?"

"Hold on there, guys," Dad said. We waited impatiently as he poured himself a cup of coffee. He gulped it down black, without his usual cream and sugar.

When Dad had gotten a little of his equilibrium back, he began to answer our questions. "First off, she's fine. At least for now. As for what happened, I can't explain it and neither can the doctors. She woke up last night, complaining about her head hurting her. She said it was as if someone was pounding her head on the ground. She's never had a migraine before and, what with her family history of stroke, I figured I'd better not take a chance. So I took her to the hospital."

"So, was it? A stroke, I mean?" Ryan asked.

Dad shook his head. "No, everything came back normal on the scans. So they're thinking it was just a migraine after all. They've got her doped up on medication. That's why she doesn't seem herself," he said.

Ryan leaned back, resting his weight on the counter. He looked relieved, like most of his questions at least had been answered.

I wasn't so easily convinced it was a migraine. "Did the scans show that it was a migraine?" I said. "I mean, how can they be a hundred percent sure?"

"They can't be," Dad said. "It's just an educated guess at this point." Dad looked beat. "I didn't get much sleep last night, so I think I'm going to go cuddle up to your Mom."

But just as he was heading out of the kitchen, he looked me up and down in my wrinkled clothes. "Looks like

120

someone else had quite a night last night." He said it in a way that wasn't amused, but a bit annoyed. Still, the message was clear. With all that was on his mind right now, the last thing he needed was for me to get into trouble.

Apparently, Dad had reason to worry about me. According to Grace, shortly after she'd made her promise, the Devil had decided to have a little fun with the Cooper that stayed behind. While the me I could remember had gone off and become case number 7892 for the State of Florida, the other me had more than a few problems. According to Grace, the Cooper Wanderman that continued to live with his mother, father and brother quickly turned into a real jerk. From what Grace had been able to gather, I'd started yelling at my parents, going as far as making a scene in a public place. My parents had blamed my behavior on the fact that I was still in love with Grace, but she had moved on. Now it made sense that my parents had freaked out that night at the restaurant.

If they only knew the truth.

But they couldn't know. I was committed to making sure that, from now on, only one Cooper Wanderman existed, the one who wasn't controlled by anyone else. And that included Lucy.

With Dad upstairs taking a nap alongside Mom, Ryan pulled out two bowls. "Lucky Charms or Cheerios?" he asked me.

Needing all the luck I could get, I picked the Lucky Charms.

Ryan balanced the two bowls, two spoons and the box of cereal in his arms. I grabbed the carton of milk from the fridge. Just as he was pouring the cereal, the phone rang. Not wanting to wake up Mom and Dad, Ryan and I nearly collided as we both ran to grab it. Ryan beat me to it.

As Ryan talked to whoever was on the other end, I took up the job of pouring the cereal and milk. My memories as a foster kid came flooding into my brain. Even though I knew those flashes of consciousness were not really part of who I was, I couldn't help but remember how many mornings I'd spent in my case worker's office eating my breakfast while she made phone calls trying to find another family who was willing to take me in.

"Don't believe what you've heard about Cooper," I'd heard the caseworker tell more than one prospective set of foster parents. "Shouldn't a kid have a chance to prove himself first before you judge him?" It was all kind of ironic now.

Ryan was off the phone.

"What's the matter?" I said when I saw the shocked look on his face.

"That was Sal," Ryan said.

"Sal? Your boss?" I suddenly remembered the name.

Ryan nodded. "He told me business is slow and he has to let me go."

I didn't know what to say. As Ryan stared down into his bowl, the only thing I did know was that all the cereal in the world wasn't going to change the facts.

CHAPTER 16

△

Maybe case number 7892 Cooper was more like me than I wanted to admit. Even though Mom was flat on her back and Ryan had lost the job that was supposed to help with his tuition, I didn't heed the warning. I called Grace anyway. Spineless as it was, I needed to hear her voice to prove to myself that the time we'd spent together wasn't just another one of Lucy's demented tricks.

Again, my call triggered her voice mail. Though I should have let it go at that, I ended up leaving a long, sappy message that I wasn't sure Grace would ever hear.

Just as Grace predicted, I spent the rest of Sunday afternoon paying for my actions. The nozzle on the outside faucet ruptured without anyone noticing. By the time Dad did notice, the whole basement was flooded with a foot of water.

To salvage our stuff, Ryan, Dad and I formed a bucket brigade with Dad at the front of the line and me at the back. It was my job to put the stuff on higher ground, but unfortunately most of the stuff was already a loss.

Mom, who'd felt well enough to get out of bed, saw the waterlogged cardboard box I was adding to the pile. "My wedding album!" she said. Her face fell. Making matters worse, two dark circles under her eyes made her look like she'd just gone eight rounds with Mike Tyson.

What Mom's wedding album was doing in the basement and not with the rest of the photo albums was beyond me. Then again, considering what we were up against, it made complete sense. After that, Mom went back to bed.

When the barbecue nearly blew up in Dad's face as he was grilling some vegetables, he blamed the weekend's calamities on a streak of bad luck. My instincts told me otherwise. Lucifer was angry. I felt it in my socks. But what really scared me was that, if Lucifer was doing this to my family, what was he doing to Grace? The fact that I could hurt her even more than I already had was killing me, and I would have happily doused myself in gasoline and set myself on fire a hundred times over if it meant I could somehow keep Grace and my family safe.

Every time I passed the phone, I had to fight the impulse to call her. It was for her own good, I told myself.

Grace wasn't the only one I wanted to talk to. If Lucy was there, I would have wrapped her fishnet stockings right around her neck. If Lucifer had split Grace and me up, then wasn't he pissed at his sister for meddling? Maybe that was why Lucy was keeping a low profile. Maybe Lucifer had scared her away or worse. Whatever the reason Lucy was incommunicado with me, I couldn't shake the feeling that I was the third point in some weird Devil's triangle.

That night I tossed and turned. My dreams flew at me like a gaggle of geese desperately flying out of the way of a plane's propeller.

The first dream took me back to the day I'd decided to burn down the school. As I snuck in, I heard the voices of little kids in the gymnasium. A weekend basketball clinic was going on. The squeals of laughing and cheering whenever one of the kids made a basket were hard to ignore. But in my dream ignoring them was exactly what I did. Regardless of the fact that the kids were there, I kept on with my original plan. With the heavy container in my hand, I could feel the sloshing of gasoline against the plastic as it bumped my leg. Though I was moving, I didn't get very far. As if I'd walked in one big circle, my walk took me right back to the gym. Just like the real version of things, I poured the gasoline. Only this time I poured it around the entrance and exit to the gymnasium. It was clear to me, even as I slept, what I was about to do. I struggled to wake myself up, but sleep, like death, had its pull on me. It wasn't until I'd already lit the match that I snapped awake.

As if the fire had leaped out of my dream and into my reality, I woke up drenched in sweat. Looking for a way to cast off the guilty feeling, I tried to find something more positive to focus on. My eyes fell on one of the trophies I'd won for playing football. The base was broad, made of marble with a gold plate with my name engraved on it, plus the name of the conference I'd won it for. The metal part of the trophy glinted in the moonlight. For a moment, I was reminded of something my third grade teacher had once said about the Statue of Liberty's torch. That torch was a sign of hope for anyone coming to this country. Thinking that trophy was my own symbol of hope, and that in a lot of ways I was new to this world, too, I fell back to sleep.

My second dream was much more pleasant than my first. Grace and I were in school. We were backstage in the auditorium, going over our lines for *King Lear*. She was dressed in a costume and her hair was all done up with little flowers woven through it. The thing was, her hair wasn't fuchsia anymore, but back to its original honey color.

"Why did you change back?" I said, touching one of the flowers in her hair.

"Because you're back," Grace explained. "Now everything can go back to the way it used to be. To the way it was supposed to be."

Since we were backstage, the tall, dark curtains blocked

us from anyone's view. Did I dare take a chance?

Leaning forward, Grace met me halfway. Against my lips, her kiss was as soft as a whisper.

"I love you, Cooper," Grace said.

"I love you," I said back. But instead of being happy, my heart felt as if it was about to break.

This time when I woke up, daylight was shining through my blinds. While my first dream had felt like a sharp pain, my second dream left me with a dull ache that was far harder to shake off.

At school, the first person I ran into was Jimmy. "Great party, huh?" Jimmy said.

A geeky freshman walked by and glanced at the two of us. His face had nothing but admiration for us.

"Yeah, pretty good," I said, reluctantly. I reminded myself that, until I could figure out a better way, all these niceties were just part of keeping up the front. I had to do this with Jimmy especially, since he was one of Blake's good buddies, an associate twice removed from Lucifer and who knew what else. The good thing about Jimmy was that he'd probably been too drunk to remember what had gone on at Blake's party.

Jimmy said, "Remember, the team doc is coming today. Maybe it's time to get you back on the field. I mean, from the way you were dodging Blake at the party on Friday, you look good to go."

Jimmy looked at me, but he wasn't so much smiling as he was smirking. Apparently he'd heard all about it.

For now I pushed the whole idea of Blake and Jimmy out of my mind. I couldn't wait to rush through my classes so I could see Grace. Only a day had gone by, and I was already starting to lose it.

But Grace wasn't at lunch and neither was Blake. By the time English came around, I was crawling up the walls. When I was first to class, Mr. Reynolds said, "You beat everyone else today, Mr. Wanderman. You must have wings."

Ordinarily, a crack like that would have bothered me, but all I wanted to do was be there when Grace showed up. That was *if* she showed up. I was starting to get more and more worried that Lucifer had done something pretty bad to her.

Since there was no assigned seating, I took the seat closest to the desk Grace always chose. But when the rest of the class started coming in, I was devastated when Grace chose a seat right next to the door, on the exact opposite side from where I was sitting.

"So tell me," Mr. Reynolds asked as he proceeded with the lesson, "As we work our way through *King Lear*, has anyone had any epiphanies?"

Twenty-five pairs of eyes stared vacantly back at Mr. Reynolds.

"Oh come on, people!" he implored. "Surely, you've learned something from what is quite arguably one of the most triumphant pieces of English literature?"

Twenty-five pairs of eyes . . . Oh, no. Scratch that. Jimmy was working a booger out of his nose probably because he didn't think anyone was watching. Twenty-four pair of eyes blinked back at Mr. Reynolds.

It wasn't my idea to raise my hand. But it seemed as if my hand decided on its own to hoist itself up and wave in the dorkiest way.

"Ah! Mr. Wanderman." Mr. Reynolds beamed. "You have something to add to the discussion? Please, please. Go on with your insights."

My insights? I was still trying to piece together everything Grace had told me about that day in the woods. What insights could I possibly have?

I glanced over at Grace. Unlike everyone else in the class, who were all waiting for me to crash and burn, Grace was looking straight ahead. It was as if she was afraid to look at me. Where was the fairness?

"Mr. Wanderman?" Mr. Reynolds insisted.

"Yeah, I did have a . . ."

"An epiphany?" Mr. Reynolds asked.

"Yeah. An epiphany," I said. I tried hard not to look over at Grace on account of I didn't want to make this any more uncomfortable than it already was. Still, I was hoping she was listening carefully to what I had to say.

"I was thinking how this whole story is really unfair," I said.

As I tried to collect my thoughts about what I'd read and about what was going on in my own life, Mr. Reynolds sat on the edge of his desk and waited patiently.

"I mean, Cordelia suffers because her father is a fool. He believes Goneril and Regan when they say they love him, but he can't look beyond their fakeness to see it's Cordelia that loves him most."

"So you find this to be unfair?" Mr. Reynolds asked.

"Well, sure. Don't you?" The way the question came out was more like the way the old Cooper used to talk to people. But Mr. Reynolds didn't seem to take offense. In fact, he sat there waiting for me to say more.

I couldn't help myself. I glanced over at Grace. She was still looking away, but I couldn't help but notice the gold threads running through the fabric of her purse that she'd plopped on top of her desk. Gold ran through Grace too, I thought to myself. Grace was special, and I couldn't imagine not having her in my life.

I finally got together in my head what I wanted to say. "I don't get why Shakespeare has to make Cordelia die in the end. She's innocent and only wanted what was best for her father."

"Shakespeare isn't the *Three Little Pigs*, Cooper," Jaimie piped in. "*King Lear* wasn't a fairy tale. It's more like life. It really sucks sometimes."

I wasn't expecting Jaimie to get in on the discussion. Everyone laughed, which, for me, was as good as agreeing.

With his finger to his lips, Mr. Reynolds looked like he was still considering what I had just said. "Mr. Wanderman brings up an important issue," he said. "Scholars have often debated that what Shakespeare intended with this play was to create a sort of discourse about whether or not life is just, or whether the world we live in is indifferent to us no matter how hard we try."

Mr. Reynolds discussed the issue for the rest of the class period. He pointed out quotes from the play and even had us read so we could experience what he called the musicality of Shakespeare's words. By the end of the class, I wasn't any more certain whether or not life really did suck.

When the bell rang, Jimmy came over to me. I tried to follow which way Grace was turning, but peering over Jimmy's shoulders was like trying to look over the rock of Gibraltar. Grace was probably better off without me hanging around her, anyway.

"That was some philosophical discussion you had going there, Coop," Jimmy said.

Picking up my books, I shrugged. The last thing I was in the mood for was hearing Jimmy's opinion on anything. Honestly, I was surprised Jimmy even knew what the word *philosophical* meant. How had he gotten in this class in the first place? With his penchant for booger diving, he'd never struck me as particularly bright. Maybe he was just one of those people who scored high on standardized tests.

Then suddenly it made sense. Jimmy was in this class to keep an eye on me. The idea that Lucifer could go into a school's mainframe and adjust a class list was over the top. Lucifer had his claws into everything. And if he had his claws in everything, maybe Grace and I weren't that special at all. Maybe there were other couples just like us that

Lucifer was messing with.

Jimmy and I walked, or I should say Jimmy escorted me, to the locker room. When we got there the place was already a zoo, complete with the stink to go with it. Blake was already dressed. In his uniform he looked more threatening than usual.

He said hi to Jimmy, gave me a friendly nod, and then continued to lace up his cleats. He acted like nothing had happened between the two of us. His coolness, which should have come as a relief, made me even more nervous.

I suited up and followed everyone else out onto to the field. As I blended in with the rest of the guys, I couldn't help but feel Blake's eyes on me. If I turned around, would his eyes look like they had on Saturday night? I knew if I glanced at him, there was a good chance that was exactly what would be staring me down. Worse, I knew no one else would see it.

So I kept my nose to the grindstone, pushing myself through the warm-ups. From all the running Ryan had forced on me, I was in pretty good shape, besting all of the other guys in the number of pull-ups I could do.

After warm-ups, I was expecting to head off to the bench like I always did, but Coach called. "Wanderman! Someone is here for you."

The fact that I had even half a hope that the someone he was talking about was Grace gave an indication of how short a string I'd put on my heart. All through warm-ups, I'd craned my neck over the huddle of flesh whenever I could to see if Grace was sitting on the bleachers watching me. She never was.

The man standing next to Coach was thin, with a rich tan. His hair was graying at the temples, but his crisp, white collared shirt and capped teeth screamed money.

"Doc wants to get a look at that ankle," Coach said.

That's right. Jimmy had told me the doctor was coming

that afternoon to check me out. I'd put it in my head that while I could make it through the warm-ups and hang out in the cafeteria with the rest of the jocks, I was definitely not jock material.

"Why don't you walk a bit so I can get a look at you," Doc suggested.

Like some kind of beauty pageant contestant, I walked in the opposite direction of Coach and Doc. As I did, I made sure to limp a little.

"Hmm," Doc said, when I came back to stand next to him.

"What do you think?" Coach asked him.

"Here, sit on this bench and put your leg up," Doc ordered.

Straddling the bench, I propped my leg up, offering my injured ankle for inspection. Limping was one thing, but I worried that once Doc actually examined my ankle, he'd find there was no real problem.

Doc made me take my cleat off. Then he rubbed two fingers over my ankle bone, pressing lightly on the skin. "Hurts, huh?" he said.

Going along with the charade, I nodded. Then Doc did the weirdest thing. Before I could protest, he gripped my heel with one hand, then with the other hand made a quick twisting motion.

"Ow!" I yelled. Though I wasn't sure if I was yelling from pain or just because the tweak to my foot had caused an audible popping sound.

"Now go ahead and try to walk," Doc said.

This time I didn't even bother putting my cleat back on. Just as I'd done before, I walked away from Doc and Coach. But this time, when I tried to limp, I couldn't.

"He looks good to go," Doc said.

Coach shook Doc's hand and thanked him.

While Coach chatted Doc up about his golf game, I

walked over the neatly trimmed turf trying to figure out why my foot refused to obey my orders to limp. Weird. My foot, like my hand in English class an hour ago, seemed to have a mind of its own.

"Ready for some real practice, Wanderman?" Coach asked.

When I looked up, the other man was gone.

"Where's Doc?" I asked Coach.

But Coach didn't answer. He was already blowing his whistle alerting the other players to fall into line.

When I looked beyond the field, in the direction of the parking lot, I thought I saw the silver glint of something. Was the Doc getting into that car? But then I realized, it wasn't a person at all, but the sun bouncing off of the car's windshield.

CHAPTER 17

Coach called out. "JV squad, you're going to run some plays against varsity."

Varsity. How I'd ever made it to this level was beyond me. I guessed there was plenty I still didn't know about myself.

Blake was the quarterback and Jimmy was the defensive lineman who stopped anyone from rushing Blake. That didn't surprise me. I was a running back. From what I could gather, it was my job to look for holes in the other team's defense.

Coach blew his whistle and I got down in my stance. This time when my fingers brushed against the neatly trimmed turf, a memory flooded my brain. Unlike the other times, this memory wasn't pictures as much as it was a feeling. Every muscle in my body tightened, and my heart jumped around like a rabbit. The feeling was like riding a roller coaster with my feet still planted on the ground.

When Alex hiked the ball to Blake, that feeling translated into movement. My legs ran without effort, zig-zagging to the left and right without having to think about it. Before I realized the opening was there, my body transported me straight past the opposing team. Call it instinct, but once I'd cleared the defensive line, I looked back for the ball.

I spotted Blake. Jimmy and the rest of them were having little difficulty keeping back the pipsqueaks on the JV team, and a clear path rested between him and me. So why wasn't he throwing the ball? Blake's eyes locked onto mine and my heart dropped. There were those beady, red eyes. The temperature must have dipped thirty degrees as the sun was blocked by a wave of clouds passing over it. Any idea my body had of moving was sucked right out of my head.

In addition to the complete paralysis I was experiencing, I started hearing things. A voice whispered in my head, "Remember. Grace is mine."

The jolt of that voice was followed through by another jolt. A short, thick-framed player barreled into my side, landing me flat on my back. As I lay there, stunned and unable to move, I watched the clouds drift over me, revealing the sun again. Mentally, I relayed a message back to Lucy and the rest of the Council. *Are you getting all this? Because if you are, can you lend me a hand here?*

All the phone lines to the afterlife must have been busy because I didn't get a response.

Even if Lucy and Saint Pete didn't respond, what about that other old guy? He'd probably need a pretty big dose of NoDoz to be of any help. No, it was crystal clear that I was on my own down here.

At least the kid who hit me had some sympathy. "You okay, Coop?" Through the face guard of the kid's helmet, I recognized the nerdy freshman from that morning.

"What's your name?" I asked him.

"Mike," the kid said. I could tell by the way he said his name that he was surprised I wasn't more pissed.

Along with everyone else, Jimmy and Blake came over to check on me, but, with Mike's help, I was already back on my feet.

"Let's not try to build Rome all in one day, Wanderman," Coach said. "Go hit the showers. The rest of you! Get back into position. You! What's your name?" Coach said pointing to Mike. "You take up Wanderman's position."

Mike glanced my way as if I was the Pope and he was waiting for me to give him a special blessing. Little did he know that he was the one doing me a favor.

In the shower, I tried to wash off the stench from the day. But no amount of soap was going to fix this. The jabs Lucifer was throwing at me had been small so far, but how long until things got worse? The thing was, I didn't know what Lucifer wanted from me. Did he honestly believe I was just going to disappear again? The question formed another in my mind. If Lucifer wanted me to disappear, then why didn't he just make it happen? Maybe Lucifer had a weak spot I just hadn't figured out yet. There was still a possibility Lucy could help.

I thought about what I'd noticed on the field that day. The clouds had covered the sun just long enough for Mike to knock into me, then they'd pushed back, allowing the sun to filter through again. Had Lucifer moved the clouds over so Lucy couldn't see what was going on?

I brushed away the whole cloud incident and went back to my original idea, that Lucifer had to have a weak spot, and it was up to me to figure out what it was.

After I dried off and put on some clean clothes, I thought of where I wanted to go next. What I wanted was to go straight to Grace's house. Even if that was remotely possible, there was no guarantee I would find her house again. The neighbor who'd told me the Sanders didn't live on his street? Grace was convinced that, like Blake, that man was another one of Lucifer's minions.

"They're everywhere, Cooper," she'd said. "You have to be careful."

Ever since Grace had helped me see that this world was my real world, something else had been weighing heavily on my mind. Something it was time for me to address.

I could have gone home and used Dad's computer, but instead I headed for the library. I asked the librarian if I could use the computer. When she told me I needed a library card to log in, I blushed. "I sort of lost mine," I said.

"Not a problem," she said, smiling. "I have a son your age, and he's always losing his keys. His name is Mike. He's a freshman on the JV team. Do you know him?"

I smiled back, not immune to the eerie coincidence. "Yeah, Mike's a good kid. He just took my spot on varsity."

The woman's face beamed with pride in a way that reminded me of my mother. "So how about we sign you up for a new library card?"

Fifteen minutes later I was sitting at a computer, typing the words Homestead School Fire into the search bar. Then I pressed enter.

One of the things I remembered about my real life was that I used to pray. Looking back, it wasn't like I really believed there was a God. Praying had been like throwing coins in a fountain. A way to get my wish. But now that I knew there was something more after you died, my way of looking at prayer was different. Instead of wishing for something to go one way or the other, I prayed I could stay strong no matter which direction it went.

What came up in the search sucked my breath away. There were at least ten stories about the fire listed. Even the *New York Times* had run a small blurb on it. I read the article from the *Times* first.

For such a famous newspaper, the reporter had sure glossed over the incident. Of course there were plenty of quotes from so-called experts. One guy was a doctor who specialized in Freudian Psychology. He claimed my burning down the school was just another example of how video game addiction in today's generation was leading to the expression of the id which had previously been held in check by the super ego. Whatever that meant. Another person quoted in the article was the vice principal. When asked for his overall impression, he spewed out some official school lingo that the school's administration would have reacted both swiftly and decisively had they viewed me as a potential problem.

Blowhards. Neither one of these so-called professionals had a clue why I'd done it. Then again, did I? Sure, I knew it had something to do with the Rasta-albino getting under my skin, but there had to be more to it.

I scrolled down the list and found another article written by a reporter for the *Homestead Daily News*. The article had interviews with some of the kids from the school, most of whom had been honest enough to admit they barely knew me. What the reporter had failed to do was ask these kids why they hadn't bothered to get to know me. While I probably didn't make it very easy on them, sitting there like a blob, my jacket zipped up to my chin and keeping everyone at an arm's length, it would have been nice if they had tried to get to know me.

Toward the end of the article, one of my old foster parents, Mrs. Murphy, had also been interviewed for the piece. Foster parents for me had been like beads on an abacus. Once it didn't work out with one, you slid that person over. There were always a long line of beads waiting, all similar, all as disillusioned with the system as the kids they took in. Mrs. Murphy was different in a lot of ways. She was up there in age, ancient, so most of the time it was like I was watching over her more than she was watching over me.

She'd had a bird. For some reason I was mesmerized by that bird. It hadn't come from the pet shop like most house birds do. Mrs. Murphy had found it in her garden one day on the verge of dying. Its wing was bent. She'd nursed it back to health, feeding it sugar water through an eye dropper and then building up its strength with worms Mrs. Murphy dug up herself.

Funny how just seeing her name in print brought it all back to me now. But there was something else curious about that bird. I remembered how one day after lunch Mrs. Murphy said, "All things got to learn to fly some time, Cooper."

At first I'd thought she was talking about me. After all, we both knew my staying with her wasn't a permanent situation. These things never were. But Mrs. Murphy was really talking about the bird.

She got up, her old knees creaking when she did. She picked up the cage and moved it to a window that was half open. She lifted the window open completely and opened the cage door. "Now you shoo off, you hear me?" Mrs. Murphy said to the bird. When the little thing refused to budge, she rattled the cage some. The bird still wouldn't go.

"That's what I was afraid of," Mrs. Murphy said. "Things get to be feeling too secure sometimes, to the point that even when they're offered freedom, they're too scared to go."

Mrs. Murphy's words struck me now, differently than how they'd struck me then.

I did another search, this time for Mrs. Murphy's phone number. When I found a listing for a Mrs. Gail C. Murphy of Homestead, Florida, I jotted it down on a piece of paper.

Outside the library, I found a quiet bench. As I plugged in the numbers on my phone, I had no idea what I would say or why I was calling her.

"Hello?" Mrs. Murphy's voice sounded no different than it had the day my case manager had come to get me. On that day, the old lady had patted my head affectionately. It was like she'd signed up for a relay and I was the baton. She was ready to pass me on to the next person in the race.

"Hello? Hello?" Mrs. Murphy repeated impatiently.

My throat suddenly felt dry. The articles on the internet should have been enough proof that I wasn't *that* boy anymore.

"Hello, Mrs. Murphy," I said.

She must have been used to getting a lot of telemarketers, because when she heard my hesitation, she quickly snapped, "Yes, come out with it, young man!"

"I was just wondering . . . the bird you used to have. Do you still have him?" I asked, tripping over my words.

Lucky for me, as long as you weren't trying to sell her something, Mrs. Murphy liked to talk. Her voice smoothed out and she chuckled. "Oh, that old bird I found in my garden? He flew away a long time ago."

On my end of the phone, I nodded as if she could see me. I was glad.

Then Mrs. Murphy said, "Cooper? Is that you?"

This time it wasn't Lucy or anyone else keeping my hand frozen in place.

Even though I wasn't talking, Mrs. Murphy filled up the silence for both of us.

"Of course you can't be Cooper, because my Cooper died in a fire down there at that school."

My Cooper. The words were darts in my heart. I imagined Mrs. Murphy sitting in her favorite chair, the one with the faded red peonies. She loved it because it had belonged to her mother. When she didn't know it, I had sunk into that chair, feeling the warm sun pouring on my face from the window next to it. Or maybe she had known all the time.

Clearing my throat, I said, "Thank you, ma'am."

I sat there for a long while after that. I thought of Mrs. Murphy with her lined face and nice smile. The truth was, not all the people who'd fostered me had been awful. A lot of them, like Mrs. Murphy, had cared. Now I saw the wall between me and them. Sure, Lucifer had set the cornerstone,

but I'd contributed to building that wall, too.
What I wanted most was to tear it down.

CHAPTER 18

As much as I didn't want to admit it, Lucifer hadn't put that can of gasoline in my hand. I had. I thought about the pain I'd caused people, Mrs. Murphy included. Even if I was under Lucifer's influence, there was no excuse.

That was what I told myself when I walked into English class the next day.

"So, is everyone prepared for their performances?" Mr. Reynolds asked the class.

Jaimie smiled her best kiss-ass smile and said, "Yes, Mr. Reynolds."

Since we'd been assigned the first scene, Mr. Reynolds directed the rest of the class to move their desks to create a circle around us. As people shifted around, I glanced over at Grace. Jaimie was chatting her up, giving her some last minute pointers. I could tell by the way Grace was nodding that she was only pretending to listen.

The door to our classroom opened and Mr. Reynolds said, "Make room, everyone!" As promised, Mrs. Lytle's English class was there to be our audience.

I cringed when I saw Blake's hulking figure walk through the door. Grace had a hard time hiding her reaction too, because when Blake leaned in for a quick smooch, she leaned the other way.

"Please limit your hormone surges to after school," Mr. Reynolds told Blake.

Blake scowled, but he avoided Grace and took a seat. I worried about what would happen to Mr. Reynolds after the class. Even without the Devil as his driving force, Blake was not one to take public ridicule lightly.

Grace stood off to the back. She seemed so small, staring at the worn linoleum. She looked like she expected the floor to open up and swallow her. Not if I could help it. Though I wasn't quite sure what I could do to stop it.

Mrs. Lytle's class was much smaller than ours because it was a remedial class. Including Blake, we had an extra six people in the room. It shouldn't have made a big difference, but Blake's presence made the room feel choked.

Mr. Reynolds was his usual enthusiastic self. "A real theater in the round!" He beamed at the arrangement. Unlike the rest of us, he was obviously looking forward to our performance.

Other than the times we'd practiced as a group, I'd barely looked at my part. To make sure we didn't trip over each other as we performed, Jaimie had drawn up a sort of map, showing us where we were supposed to stand while we said our lines.

Not only was Blake staring me down now, but so was Jaimie. I looked around and realized I wasn't in the right spot. Blake snickered as Jaimie grabbed me by the arm and positioned me, like a mannequin, in the place I was supposed to be.

"Are you going to put him in a dress, too?" Blake asked Jaimie.

The only one who laughed was Jimmy.

"Anytime you're ready," Mr. Reynolds said to our group. I was starting to think the reason he was so keen on us acting was because he liked watching us bump into each other.

Well, we certainly gave Mr. Reynolds plenty to laugh about. The kid who played Kent, whose name I still didn't know, looked down at his map and then took four steps forward toward Jimmy. Jaimie rolled her eyes and pointed directly to the map like that was obviously not what she'd had in mind.

After Kid-Kent delivered his first line, Jimmy stood there, shifting nervously from foot to foot and not saying anything. Though I could still feel the heat of Blake's eyes against my back, I couldn't help but smirk at poor Jimmy. If Attila the Hun had a girly bladder, Jimmy would be him.

The more Jimmy squirmed, the redder Jaimie's face turned. Glancing over to where Grace stood behind Mr. Reynold's podium, I noticed that even she couldn't stop herself from smiling. The soft curl of her lips brought me immediately back to the time we'd spent in her room. The feeling of her body, curled up perfectly next to mine, still lingered. Sometimes I thought I'd just imagined the sensation. If things had gone normally for us and we'd been like any other high school couple, there would be no problem with me standing right next to Grace now, possibly even holding her hand. Well, Mr. Reynolds might have had something to say about that.

And once we were done with the Shakespearean fiasco, I would have been able to walk Grace to her bus just like any other boyfriend would. I'd even get to give her a kiss good-bye without the threat of everyone around us being instantly engulfed in a wall of fire.

"Um, Mr. Wanderman?"

Looking up from my daze, I saw that Mr. Reynolds was pointing at me. What Mr. Wanderman did he see, I wondered? Then I remembered the play.

With a lot of help from Jaimie, Jimmy had somehow managed to get through his lines. Jaimie was sitting on the top of a desk, looking miserable. Mrs. Lytle's class looked bored.

Reminding myself I was no longer in the business of making excuses, and hating the idea of publicly crashing and burning in front of Blake, I took a breath and cleared my mind.

By some miracle, the first few words came to me. "Attend the Lords of France and Burgundy, Gloucester," I said.

As if I'd given her another chance to hope, Jaimie perked up. At the mention of his character's name, Jimmy stared at me in a panic. For a guy who had no problem spending his days plowing through a pile of muscle, Shakespeare had managed to reduce Jimmy to a scared mouse. He looked at Jaimie, waiting for her to bail him out again.

Angry that Jimmy had squashed what little momentum we had going, Jaimie fed Jimmy his next line. "I shall, my lord," she said.

"Um, yeah. I shall, my lord," Jimmy said. But instead of saying it to me, Jimmy said it back to Jaimie.

Everyone started laughing. Mr. Reynolds slipped his hand over his mouth, doing a poor job of hiding his amusement.

"Get out of there, you idiot," Jaimie said, waving Jimmy off our invisible stage.

Jimmy tucked his tail between his legs and found refuge next to the bookshelf in the far corner. Jaimie looked crushed, her rock-solid GPA sinking before her eyes.

The poor girl. We both knew how it felt to have what was most important to us taken away.

Mr. Reynolds cleared his throat, a clear signal that it was now or never for me.

Even though Mr. Reynolds had, as he'd put it "judiciously edited" our lines, what I had to say next was still a pretty good mouthful. Remembering Grace's advice that I should think about what the words meant, I took a breath and stepped into it.

This was the part where King Lear announces his plan to step down from his throne and divide his kingdom evenly. I delivered the first line. "Meanwhile we shall express our darker purpose–"

Blake's eyes were still focused on me. The heat from his glare was withering. Was he trying to spontaneously combust me into a pile of ash right there and then? Beads of sweat formed on my forehead and Grace looked at me, concern clear on her face. She took a tiny step forward, a step I doubted had anything to do with Jaimie's map. This small gesture on Grace's part was enough for Blake to turn the heat up even higher. Coursing through my body, it was overwhelming, but no one else seemed to notice.

No one except Grace. She pulled back, retracing her step. The heat in my body subsided enough for me to find my breath again. Lucifer, through Blake, was breaking down my choice for me. Choose Grace and cease to exist.

"We're waiting," Jaimie said. At this point she was beyond demoralized and just plain bitchy.

Mr. Reynolds leaned forward. He stared at me intently, his hand on his chin. His eyes, I noticed for the first time, were blue and piercing. He looked at me curiously.

Choose Grace and cease to exist. But hadn't I already seen that life without Grace was like not existing at all?

How the words came to me I wasn't sure. I assumed the force that had helped me find my stride when running alongside Ryan, the same force that had helped me to play football, was the same force at work now. Maybe this force was the real me.

The words came. "Know that we have divided in three our kingdom, and 'tis our fast intent to shake all cares and business from our age . . ."

After that, I had a few little screw ups, but, just like

she'd done with Jimmy, Jaimie helped me out. Surprisingly, our group was getting by.

When it was Jaimie's turn to do her part as Goneril, someone whispered *gonorrhea* under their breath. To her credit, Jaimie wasn't knocked off course. She recited her lines perfectly, and when she was done, her accomplishment left a shimmer of happiness on her face.

I couldn't help myself. Seeing Jaimie happy about what she'd accomplished touched a nerve in me. I wanted that feeling, not just for me, but especially for Grace. She deserved it.

Standing up straight and squaring my shoulders, I imagined Blake's position as he sat behind me and slightly to the left. If I took him by surprise, possibly in the middle of reciting my next lines . . .

In the middle of that thought, I was again slammed by a sheet of oppressive heat. That time I really thought I had burst into flames. I rocked on my feet, the high temperature making me dizzy. If I fell on my face, I doubted my hands would be able to protect me, for they too felt paralyzed, as if Blake had lashed them to my body.

This time I refused to look up. If there was a chance Grace couldn't see what was happening to me, there was a chance she wouldn't do anything, therefore keeping her safe.

"Would someone please open a window," Mr. Reynolds said. He was now fanning himself with a piece of folded up paper.

Was he feeling it, too? Maybe not to the same extent, but I was grateful someone else was sharing my pain.

The open window did the trick. A crisp autumn breeze found its way into the classroom. Behind me, I heard Blake shift in his chair. A few kids yawned, seemingly oblivious to what was going on. If they only knew how freakishly close they'd come to seeing a real live person burst into flames.

After Jaimie was done professing her love for me, her

fictional father, it was Grace's turn to deliver her lines. For the first time, I felt immensely grateful to Jaimie for choreographing our performance. Now Grace had a reason for standing close to me. Whether Blake realized that this was just part of the play or he was getting bored, my body temperature did not spike up more than it normally would have with Grace standing so close.

As Grace spoke her lines, I fantasized that the two of us were back in her room again, safe and protected.

"What shall Cordelia speak? Love, and be silent," Grace said.

It was the first time I really listened to the words. The lines spilled out of Grace's mouth with so little effort. For the first time I realized that, like the code we'd used when we were little kids, Grace was trying to speak to me through Shakespeare.

I wanted more, but Grace said nothing else. This was because it was my turn to speak. Jaimie got sick of waiting around for me to say my lines, so she said them for me. Again there was some laughter, but I ignored it. Standing there in the happy glow of Grace's eyes was more than enough for me.

After Jaimie said my part, it was time for Lana to say her lines as Lear's other daughter, Regan.

"I am made of that self-mettle as my sister," she said. Then she proceeded to wiggle over to me. To a lot of hooting and hollering, Lana slid her hand down the front of my shirt, feeling me up.

Mrs. Lytle looked uncomfortable and Mr. Reynolds said, "Now, now, Lana. Remember, Regan is Lear's daughter."

"I'm just professing my love," Lana said impishly. This remark invited another round of hooting, and even Jimmy came out from around the bookcase to whoop it up.

Mr. Reynolds smirked. "Okay, okay. Let's get on with

it, already."

Lana bowed, her low-cut shirt giving the audience more than they were expecting. Then she reluctantly went back to her assigned spot.

Because it's human nature to turn everything into a competition, everyone waited to see what Grace would do to one-up Lana. All I cared about was that Grace was still standing next to me.

For the first time I wished Mr. Reynolds hadn't cut the lines for this scene, reducing our time together. When Grace did recite her next few lines, though, it was as if Shakespeare had known that someday two average kids like us would need his words more than air.

"Unhappy that I am, I cannot heave my heart into my mouth. I love Your Majesty according to my bond, no more nor less," Grace said.

Blake scraped his chair against the floor. Another warning, I knew. I ignored the shrill, metallic sound, and instead melted into Grace's words. Both Shakespeare and Grace were right. Grace and I had a bond.

I was sure there was more. Hoping, maybe. I didn't want the words to come from Jaimie, though. Grace needed to hear the words in my heart.

Before I could do or say anything, the bell rang.

"Wait!" Jaimie yelled. Even Jaimie's bossiness couldn't stop the tide of kids rushing out of the class.

Jaimie turned to Mr. Reynolds, who was busy shutting the window. "We didn't get to finish," she complained.

I searched Grace's face. In that split second as I tried to figure out what to do, Blake stepped up, lassoed his arm around Grace and pulled her into the current flooding out the door.

CHAPTER 19

Out in the hall, the animals were escaping the zoo. The energy was nuts, with guys high-fiving each other and couples squeezing in a little make-out time before they had to run off to catch their separate buses home.

I rocked on my toes, trying to see over the ocean of crashing hormones. It was useless. Blake had swept Grace out of there, fast.

I stood there, my back against someone's locker, the knob of the lock jamming me in the kidneys. I felt lost, but then I remembered the way Grace had looked at me when she'd said she loved me. While I was happy, I was also scared that she'd taken the risk, especially with Blake front and center like he was.

As I tried to figure out what had made Grace take such a chance, I caught sight of a couple a few lockers down. The rest of the crowd had begun to thin out, but they were too busy playing tonsil hockey to notice the rest of the world. Disgusted, I watched the guy coyly work his hand up the side of the girl's body.

"Hey! Do you think you can take your groping somewhere else?" I growled, startling the two of them.

The girl looked down at her feet and then at her boyfriend. The guy, an underclassman from the looks of him, frowned, but based on our size difference, he didn't chance it. Instead, he tugged at his girlfriend's arm, dragging her away.

I was even angrier now. Not with them, but with myself. While I knew why the sight of them had pissed me off, it still didn't give me the right to direct it toward them.

"There you are!"

From behind me, a girl's voice. But when I turned around, it was only Jaimie.

"Oh," I said.

"Oh my God," she said. "Can you, like, possibly contain your enthusiasm anymore?"

"Sorry."

"Yeah, well. I thought you'd like to know that Mr. Reynolds thought we were great. He gave us all A+'s."

"Uh huh."

Jaimie stared at me like I was some rare genetic mutant. I thought she was going to get on my case again, but instead she said, "Cheer up, Cooper. You'll find a way to get her back."

Jaimie flashed me a smile. Smiling wasn't something Jaimie did often, so I'd never noticed the silver braces on her teeth.

"See ya," Jaimie said.

"Yeah. See ya," I said back.

For a girl who always had her head in a book, she read me pretty well. The thing was, if my feelings for Grace were that obvious to Jaimie, there was no hope that they were hidden from the prying eyes of Lucifer, or Blake, for that matter.

A shudder ran through me as the anger I'd been feeling changed to fear. Now I saw why Grace had taken the risk. She was afraid she'd never have the chance again. Did Grace think Lucifer was going to find a way to keep us permanently apart?

Right before the final bell rang, Principal Brillstein made an announcement over the loud speaker. "Just a reminder that there is a mandatory meeting of all varsity football players today."

As if the Devil himself was standing behind me, a warm blast of air brushed the back of my neck. I headed for the gym.

By the time I got to the locker room, the guys were already suited up and heading out to the field. Like a lot of things right then, football was something I did just because I didn't see any way around it. Also, my parents and Ryan seemed to care a lot about my doing well at school, and football was a part of that.

Coach was busy talking to some guy when I trotted onto the field. Everyone milled around, waiting for Coach to start practice. I scanned the bleachers. There were a lot more people than usual. It was a nice day, with the last bit of summer hanging on. That could have been the reason for the larger than usual crowd.

When I caught sight of the shock of fuchsia hair on one of the top bleachers, my mouth went dry. Grace was alone. Even from this distance, I saw something noticeably stiff in the way she sat. Her hands rested in her lap, and there was no sign of her notebook. My first instinct was to wave. Then I glanced over at Blake. I could see he was just waiting to turn up the heat. I resisted. For now, I had to be satisfied with knowing that Grace was in sight and safe.

Coach came around to the rest of us. The man he'd been busy talking to joined him. Now that I could see his face, I didn't like the looks of him. He looked at us hungrily, his gaze skipping over us as if we were some all-you-can-eat buffet.

"Fall in!" Coach yelled. We dutifully formed a loose semi-circle around the two men.

"I want to introduce all of you to Mr. Sam Jaeger. Sam

151

and I go a long way back. He also happens to be a college scout. I've been talking to him about some of you, and he wants to see what you've got."

Apparently this was some big deal, because people started whispering excitedly. They shifted their bodies, standing on the balls of their feet, attempting to look a lot less slouchy.

I thought of Ryan. This was how it had happened for him. A scout had come to Pace and offered him his so-called free ride. Partly because of what had happened to Ryan and partly because I had bigger worries on my mind, I tuned out the rest of what Coach had to say.

Hoping Blake wouldn't notice, I glanced back up at the bleachers. Other than for her hair, Grace could have been any other girl sitting there. But she wasn't. With all that Grace had sacrificed for me, it was a wonder there weren't a bunch of rainbows arching over the spot where she sat. If I ever got the chance, I'd have to talk to Lucy about doing something special for Grace.

Lucy. Given how much I had on my mind, I'd forgotten about our little deal. With just a little over two weeks left, I wondered what she would do if I didn't help Grace. Or maybe I just didn't want to think about it. Even if I did find a way to release Grace from Lucifer's grasp, that only meant I'd earn my place in Heaven. What would Lucy do if I didn't want to go back? What could she do? As hoity-toity and all powerful as Lucy made herself out to be, it was clear Lucy was afraid of her brother.

All the time I was puzzling over it, Coach had been yammering on. He shouted out the plays we were going to run through. Like my lines for *King Lear*, I didn't have them memorized either.

We were told to break down into our squads. Whatever that witch doctor had done to my foot, there was no way I was getting out of it. Poor Mike. He looked down in the dumps that he wasn't going to get his chance. If it was at all realistic, I would have gladly sprained my ankle all over again to give him his shot.

Yeah, if I ran real hard on my ankle, maybe I could pop it out of alignment or whatever happened to ankles when they got sprained. As I fantasized about it, a plan started taking shape in my head.

Grace and I would run away together! Sure, Lucifer would catch up to us eventually, but by putting a little distance between us and Blake, maybe Lucy would have a chance to intervene. Just a day or two away from here might be all we needed.

I took up my position. A little too close for comfort, Blake stood to my right and Jimmy diagonal to me. It was like being a cow in one of those inhumane dairy farms where they keep the animals caged up side by side without any chance of escaping. I knew Blake wanted to rip me to pieces. Luckily, teammates weren't allowed to do that to each other.

Coach blew his whistle and someone hiked the ball to Blake. Just like the day before, my feet had a mind of their own. Without thinking, I ran to my left, finding an open pocket. Free from the rest of the pack, my feet padded the turf, the goal post looking like a capital H in the distance.

In my head, I knew it wasn't good. I willed the pigskin away, actually hoping that someone would plow me into the field.

When I looked back at the offensive line, my heart dropped. As if someone had used a compass to project the perfect arc, the ball zoomed through the air, landing with an audible *thunk* into my waiting arms. I was completely open.

The last thing I saw before turning around and heading for the goal line was the smug smile on Blake's face and the light pink cast to his eyes.

As if someone had written a script for a movie titled *Football Hero* with me in the leading role, I ran past the thirty—, the twenty—, and finally, the ten-yard line. Just for a little added drama, some of the guys on the opposing side lunged at me, but I expertly avoided them. As I made the touchdown, I heard familiar banter in my ears. That time there was no question as to who was laughing at me.

Coach blew his whistle. I looked behind me. Aside from Blake's obvious grin, Sam Jaeger also looked like the hours on the all-you-can-eat buffet had just been extended. Sweat poured down my face, and I took off my helmet. Looking up at the bleachers again, I saw that Grace was no longer alone. Ryan was sitting next to her. He looked at the field and then said something to Grace. For someone with a grudge, Ryan looked a little too chummy for my taste.

Coach and Sam Jaeger walked over to me. "That was really impressive, young man," Sam said to me.

Shrugging like it was no big deal (after all, it *was* no big deal), I said, "Thanks."

Sam stood a little too close. As he spoke, his words about football and playing for his school rolled right over me.

"Yeah, thanks," I said as Sam pressed his business card into my hand. I promised him I would have Mom and Dad give him a call only because I thought that would get rid of him faster.

Sam said he had to go, and Coach walked him off the field. As they left, I looked back up at the bleachers. Neither Ryan nor Grace was sitting there. My eyes scanned the whole length of the field, but it was as if the two of them had just disappeared.

After Sam was gone, Coach came back. He still had plenty of drills he wanted us to run through. Like Pavlov's dog, the minute Coach blew his whistle, I got into line. The point of the drill was to improve our agility by running through tires that had been set out in a long row.

As I waited my turn, Mike came up from behind me.

"That's really awesome about the college scout being after you, man. I bet he's going to offer you a scholarship to come play at his school."

Mike was a nice kid and all, but I really didn't want to get into it.

"I just hope you like snow." Mike laughed.

I was barely paying attention. With two more guys ahead of me, all I wanted to do was run through my drill and get out of there. Maybe if Blake took some time in the shower, I could catch up to Grace and talk to her about running away.

One more guy to go and then it was my turn. But then Mike's comment hit me.

"What did you mean by you 'hope I like snow'?" I said, turning around.

"What? Didn't you know? Sam Jaeger is a college scout for the University of Juneau."

"Juneau?"

"In Alaska," Mike said.

Alaska?

When it was my turn to run the drill, I fell over the first set of tires, landing on my knees.

"Wanderman! Do it again!" Coach yelled.

As I got back into line, Blake was already heading for the showers. He looked back at me and laughed. I knew he'd made me fall down on purpose.

I got back in line and tried it again.

"What is with you, Wanderman?" Coach said, clearly disgusted. That was nothing compared to how disgusted I felt with myself.

By the time I got through the drill, I was the last person to the locker room. Blake was gone.

CHAPTER 20

I tore off my cleats and ran to find Grace. Instead, I ran right into Ryan.

"There you are," he said, smiling. "I had a little bit of time and figured I'd come down and see you practice." Ryan had a whole lot of time on his hands. Time he should have been using to find a job.

"Yeah, well, I'm kind of busy," I said, trying to get around him. Every time I tried, he got in my way.

"Busy. Right." Ryan delivered a little one-two punch with his words.

We might have been brothers, but I was starting to feel a little cramped, like Ryan was watching me a little too closely.

Blake and Grace had to be long gone by now, no thanks to Ryan who seemed hell bent on standing in my way. A familiar sensation boiled up inside of me. "What's your problem, anyway?"

Ryan shook his head. "You just don't get it, do you?"

"Get what?"

"A second chance doesn't come around every day, Boomer. Don't throw it away."

At first, I thought Ryan was talking about Grace, but then I remembered the night at the restaurant and how Ryan had been so quick to tattle to my parents. In Ryan's mind, my only hope at a second chance in life didn't include Grace.

"What did you say to her?" I demanded.

Ryan looked at me. "I didn't say anything to Grace she didn't already know. Sometimes two people are toxic together, Boomer. It's better for them to stay away from each other. Grace agreed."

"You don't know what you're talking about!" I said. If I didn't know any better, I would have thought Ryan was on Lucifer's side. But Ryan was filled to the brim with his own anger. He didn't need Lucifer to light the match.

As if he was out to prove that he knew better than me, Ryan pointed to the huge glass case he was standing in front of. While I'd passed it every day on my way to the gym, I'd never really taken a close look at the awards locked up inside.

"See that one? I got it for breaking the record in the hundred-meter dash." The trophy Ryan pointed to was the biggest one in the case, big enough to hold a dead person's ashes – a really big, dead person.

"And that one's from Regionals. And the one over here is when our team won the title at the Shore Conference."

Ryan wasn't focused on me anymore. He was pressing his palms against the glass case, remembering. From what I could tell, Ryan was responsible for a good portion of the awards.

Fed up, I shoved my hands into the pocket of my jacket. My right hand touched the small square card from Sam Jaeger. The college scout, Ryan talking to Grace, and now this.

"Is that why you showed up today? Because you knew the scout was coming?"

Ryan shrugged his shoulders. "Coach called me. I knew you wouldn't tell Mom and Dad."

I couldn't deal with this right now. Before Ryan could

plan out my life for me – plans that did not include Grace – I headed outside.

"Boom! Boomer!" Ryan kept calling my name as I stalked across the parking lot. He might have been a good head taller than me, with a lot longer stride, but I managed to keep ahead of him. I thought about walking home, but that would have just slowed me down more.

Ryan didn't bother giving me the keys. Good thing. With how I was feeling, I would have driven the two of us right off the next cliff. Whatever Ryan claimed to be true, there was no way Grace had agreed that it was better we stay away from each other.

Ryan revved the motor and I slumped down in the passenger side. Maybe Ryan finally got the message I didn't want to talk, because he shut up.

The problem with being the new, improved Cooper was that, when it would have been easier to stick with just one feeling, other more complicated feelings had a tendency to float to the surface, muddying the waters. That time, it was guilt.

I thought about how things might have been different for Ryan had I not caused all the problems I had. If Mom and Dad hadn't been so concerned about me, then maybe things might have been different for him.

Another thing I'd never considered before was what would have happened if Grace had said no to Lucifer. What if she hadn't sacrificed her life for me and I'd been just zapped into oblivion? Maybe everyone would have been better off.

All the way home we drove in silence, but before I could get out of the car, Ryan said, "Boomer."

Though I didn't always agree with him, he was my brother. "What?" I said, holding myself in my seat for a few seconds longer than I wanted to.

"You know I have to tell Mom and Dad about Sam

Jaeger, don't you?"

In that split second I realized something. As mad as Ryan got, he'd never stopped calling me Boomer. It was because, underneath it all, we were brothers.

"Yeah. I know," I said.

But just like love had forced Ryan into his decision, I was equally convinced about what I had to do.

Ryan didn't have a chance to rat me out. When we got in the house, no one was home. Ryan disappeared into the basement, most likely to deal with the real world by disappearing into the fake world of video games. I took off for my room.

As I called Grace, my hands shook. Stay confident, I told myself. We can sort this out. Any fears she had would subside once I told her about my plan. Truthfully, I didn't have the details worked out, but all we needed was each other. The rest would follow.

But when Grace picked up the phone, I felt the solid wall between us right away.

"Hi, Cooper," she said even before I'd said hello. Her voice sounded stiff, not at all like the girl who'd lain in my arms for hours. Every time Grace had told me she loved me, I'd felt like a drunk who'd fallen off the wagon. One whispery I love you and I couldn't get enough.

"You knew it was me?" I asked.

"Who else would it be?" Grace laughed, but her laugh wasn't a happy one. Something inside of me started to splinter. I tried to hold onto the pieces.

"I just talked to Ryan," I said. This wasn't even what I'd wanted to talk to her about. I wanted to tell her about my plan and about how much I loved her and with a little faith . . .

Instead, I found myself being that scrappy, scared kid who, when cornered, didn't know what to do except fight.

"You can't listen to them. Any of them! I won't let you

do this again, Grace!"

"Cooper," Grace said, but I didn't let her finish. All those years of beating someone to the punch before they could land me flat on my face was coming back.

Choosing my words a bit more carefully, I said, "I just talked to Ryan and I don't get it. He told me you said you didn't want to talk to me anymore. But I said he had to be wrong about that. I mean, that's just a cover up, right? Until we can figure this all out?"

On the other end, Grace hesitated. In my heart I prayed that this was a sign she was surprised or maybe even angry with Ryan for twisting her words around.

"Ryan's right," Grace said. "I did tell him that."

The whole afternoon came racing back to me – Grace standing within arm's reach, the way she looked at me as she recited those words. Had I only imagined the bond between us?

"You're just doing this to protect me. But we can do this. You just have to have faith in me," I said.

Another pause. I squirmed in my chair, hoping there was still something in me that people could rest their faith in.

"Don't I deserve a chance?" I was practically begging now. "When I saw you that first day with your pink hair and weird piercings . . ." This was not coming out the way I wanted it to. "What I mean, Grace, is that . . ."

"I just can't do this anymore, Cooper."

I didn't need Lucifer to supply me with venom. I had plenty stored up in me to go around. "He got to you, didn't he?" I said, accusingly. But even I didn't know who *He* was. Was I talking about Lucifer? Or Blake, or Ryan? What did it matter? I could feel Grace slipping away.

There was no hesitation in Grace's response now. "No, Cooper. This is my decision."

Out of everything, I realized this was what I'd been

afraid of most of all. The girl I'd loved and lost and loved was slipping away again. Only now it wasn't Lucifer tearing us apart. This time it was Grace choosing to step away on her own.

And who could blame her?

"Today was a mistake," she said.

The disappointment I'd heard in Ryan's voice a little while ago was nothing compared to the not-so-hidden message Grace was sending me now. What she really meant was that *I* was the mistake. Grace was finally realizing that on account of me, she'd wasted her own chance at eternity.

On the other end of the phone, I heard Grace sigh. This was a different sigh than the one I'd listened to contentedly while we'd been cuddled together in her room.

"I'm sorry, Cooper," she said. The phone went dead, and whatever few splinters I'd been trying to hold onto exploded into a powdery nothingness.

I sat there, the phone curled up in my hand like a dead animal. The silence settled in and my heart rattled around in my chest. Compared to Grace telling me to go away, dying felt like winning the lottery.

I wasn't allowed to wallow for long. The sound of my father's voice startled me out of my limbo. "Ryan! Cooper! Boys, are you home?"

At first I ignored him. I was hoping that by waiting it out, Lucy would have time to swoop down and reclaim me.

CHAPTER 21

When Dad yelled again, he only said my name. It figured. Good son Ryan was probably front and center. No doubt he'd already spilled his guts about the college scout, too. Not that I cared. Alaska. Hell. It was all the same at that point.

Dad yelled up again. His voice sounded downright frantic. That was when I looked at the clock.

Downstairs, I found Dad in the living room. Ryan was sitting on the couch, a half-eaten sandwich set down on the coffee table in front of him.

"What are you doing home?" I asked Dad. Somehow, from the way he was pacing, I knew this had nothing to do with my football career.

Dad stopped pacing and frowned. Then I heard it. More quiet. The normal sounds of life, like the clanking of glasses coming out of the dishwasher or the tapping of keys at the computer, weren't there. This quiet ripped me apart in a whole other way.

"Where's Mom?" I asked.

"Your mother had another bad headache today." The pain I saw locked away in his face was enough to rock me off my feet. "This time there was blood." He rubbed his hand through his hair, and I knew it wasn't a small amount of blood he was talking about.

"Where is she?" Ryan asked.

"They rushed her to the hospital. They took a scan of her brain and . . ." Dad couldn't bring himself to say the rest, though from the look on his face, I knew it had to be really bad.

Outside, I could have sworn that I heard the scritch, scritch, scratching of a pack of hungry, horned wolves clawing their way in. Lucy hadn't come, but her brother had.

Dad sat down next to Ryan. There was still more space on the couch, but I stayed standing. Somehow I didn't feel like I deserved that spot.

"I don't get it," Ryan said. For such a big guy, he looked awfully small sitting there. Even the bite marks on his half-eaten peanut butter and jelly sandwich looked dainty now.

"They don't know anything for sure yet," Dad said. "They have to do more tests." But I could tell by the way he said it, he was trying to be optimistic for the two of us.

As the two of them sat there stunned, my gaze was drawn to the floor. Next to the coffee table sat one of Mom's many photo albums. Picking it up, I saw that a Post-it note with one of Mom's shopping lists was tucked into one of the pages.

The page was filled with pictures of all of us on a trip to Maine. One of the pictures showed Ryan and me sitting at a picnic bench at some hokey little roadside restaurant. Fishing nets decorated the worn shaker shingles of the little hut, and there was a picture of some guy standing over a big pot of boiling water. Another picture showed Ryan and me, both of us wearing lobster bibs, mugging for the camera. We were pretend dueling, each of us holding a red lobster claw in our hands as if they were swords.

For the life of me, I didn't remember that day or any other detail of that trip. Lucifer had erased so much of who I'd been, and now he was trying to take away what was left. That included my mother.

"Can we go see her?" Ryan asked Dad.

Dad grabbed his keys. At the hospital, the receptionist directed us to the oncology floor.

"Oncology?" Ryan seemed stunned. "Isn't that for people with cancer?"

Dad didn't answer.

When we walked into her room, Mom said, "Oh! My babies are here!" The male nurse who was fussing with her IV nodded at us and then proceeded to punch some numbers into the electronic box connected to the pole.

When the nurse left, I didn't look at him all that closely. What I did notice was the weak smile on Mom's face. Her skin, which had been so pink and lively the day before, now looked as washed out and pale as the hospital gown she wore. I'd seen plenty of ghostly complexions. It wasn't good.

Mom lifted her arms and waved us close. As big as Ryan was, he melted into her embrace like a newborn. When she let go, he walked to the other side of the room, looking away so we wouldn't see him crying.

"Cooper," Mom said, my name catching in her throat.

She started coughing and Dad practically spilled the entire pitcher of water sitting on Mom's rollaway table in his hurry to pour her a glass. As he lifted the plastic cup to her lips, the knot in my stomach tightened. As easy as it was to blame Lucifer for this, I couldn't shake the feeling that it was just as much my fault. Grace had warned me that if I didn't keep my feelings in check, I'd be giving Lucifer a free pass to do whatever he wanted to me and to the people I loved.

Mom drank her water, which took away her cough long enough for her to say what she needed to say. Again, she reached out her hand and waved me close. I sat on the edge of Mom's bed, but that didn't satisfy her.

"Give your mamma a hug," she said.

Careful not to knock into her tubes, I did what she

wanted me to do and squeezed in next to her on the narrow bed. As I mentally counted all the blips and beeps of Mom's monitor, it scared me to realize how fragile life was. When I thought about all that Lucifer had taken from me, I wanted to explode. What good was that, though? In another lifetime, losing control hadn't gotten me anywhere.

Mom took a breath. The life was still inside of her. It was up to me to make sure it stayed there.

Over the next few days, the more I resisted the temptation to talk to Grace, the better Mom got. A few more days went by and Mom's cheeks pinked up. She still needed the tubes, but her appetite was better and she could manage to hold down a piece of toast.

So that was the trade-off. Mom's heart for mine. The solution wasn't perfect, but for then, at least until Lucy decided to step up to the plate, it was all I had.

When I went to visit Mom in the hospital, she insisted I sit on her bed so she could stroke my face or my hand. Even with the small bits of progress she had made, the doctor had warned us that Mom was not out of the woods yet. And when I thought of those woods, and the black shadows lurking there, I felt the weight of Mom's recovery squarely on my shoulders.

Friday afternoon after school when I went to visit her, Mom didn't say much. Instead, she kept stroking my hand, plucking my fingers lightly as if they were piano keys. If she'd ever done that when I was little, the memory had been obliterated from my mind.

"You know it's going to be okay," I said, trying my best to comfort her. "I mean a person like you, you've got it in the bag."

"In the bag?" she said.

"You know. Heaven. First class all the way." I shot my hand out in the air, pretending it was a plane.

Her eyes grew large and, from her expression, I realized

what a dope I was to say such a thing. I had the poor woman already dead and buried. "I'm sorry. That didn't come out the way I meant it."

Mom smiled. "No need to be sorry, Cooper. I appreciate your . . . um . . . belief in me. And your wisdom."

"Yeah, right. Like I know it all," I said.

"Don't write yourself off so soon," she said.

Mom continued to pick out a silent melody on my fingers. The memory of being a kid tossed around in the foster system hit me all over again. Though I hadn't wanted to admit it back then, a mother like her could've made a real difference. I was back where I belonged, and I realized what I'd been running away from with Mrs. Murphy and some of the other people who had really tried with me. Loving someone came with a risk. There was always a chance you might lose them.

Mom tried to pull herself up in bed. I helped her by arranging her pillow so it gave her some support.

"I really should go," I said. "You look like you could use some sleep."

Mom shook her head fiercely. She pointed to the spot next to her and I dutifully sat.

It must have taken all her strength, but Mom spilled what was on her mind. "You know there was a while when your father and I thought we'd lost you," she said.

At the mention of that time, my back stiffened. Both Ryan and Grace had mentioned what I'd been like after Lucifer had done his deed and had literally split me in two, but Mom and Dad never spoke about it. Sometimes I got the feeling that they tiptoed around that time, afraid to trip a landmine.

"You know what the worst thing about it was?" Mom started coughing, but she waved away my offer of a glass of water. It couldn't be good for her, the rehashing of old pain. I knew from experience that physical pain didn't compete

166

with the pain we held in our hearts. Still, Mom had a need to get it off her chest.

When she'd caught her breath, Mom continued, "The worst part was that you not only gave up on me and your dad and the rest of the world, you gave up on yourself as well."

She took hold of my hand. As tight as she tried to make her grasp, her hand still felt way too breakable. "Please promise me you'll never give up on yourself again."

My heart raced ahead of the blips and beeps on Mom's heart monitor. How could one person keep all those promises? For days, I'd been wondering about something. All that time I'd been blaming Lucifer for turning me into a spineless whiner, but maybe I'd wanted to take the easy way out.

Mom coughed and I patted her back. "It's okay. I'm right here," I told her. I refused to take the easy way out again.

The weekend was more of the same. Ryan and I drove the Camaro over to the hospital where we hung out in Mom's room until the nurse threw us out.

On the way out to the parking lot, Ryan handed over the keys. "You drive. I'm beat."

We were just a few blocks from the hospital and Ryan was already snoring in the seat next to me. On the way home, I recognized the turn for Grace's street. With Ryan still passed out, I figured what harm would come of just taking a little detour past Grace's house. But the minute the idea flashed into my head, Ryan grimaced and started talking in his sleep.

"Fire the gun!" he yelled. Whatever he was dreaming about sounded like a nightmare.

As we passed Grace's street, Ryan settled down, his face relaxing.

On Monday morning, Dad gave us the update on Mom's condition. "The doctors are still baffled," he said.

Ryan stared into his bowl of cereal. "What does that mean?" He held his spoon with an iron grip. Besides the dimple in his right cheek, I recognized myself in him. It was all getting to be too much for Ryan, and I knew what could happen to a person when all of those things came to a boil.

"Well, she's not out of the woods yet," Dad cautioned. "But it may mean that if she continues to get better, then there's really no reason for them to keep her in the hospital."

Apparently, this small ray of hope was enough to bring the boil down to a simmer. I watched as the muscles in my brother's shoulders, the ones he had earned from working out, relaxed a bit. As Ryan gobbled up a heaping spoonful of Lucky Charms, I couldn't help but feel as if everything now rested on my shoulders.

Over the week that followed I pretended to be a normal high school senior. I went to school every day, did my homework, and when I wasn't doing stuff around the house to help Dad, I visited Mom in the hospital. The doctors still wanted to keep an eye on her, but we were all hopeful that she'd be released soon. While Ryan and Dad thought it was all up to Mom's body to do the right thing, the irony was that Mom's condition had nothing to do with her.

Though it was breaking me apart not to be able to talk to Grace, I maintained my self-control, allowing myself a glance here and there whenever Mr. Reynolds called on her to read a passage from *Julius Caesar*. With a little over a week left until the deal with Lucy reached its expiration date, I didn't know how many more glances I had left.

"Come, come, Miss Sanders. Put some mustard in it!" Mr. Reynolds said as Grace read listlessly. Maybe I was grasping at straws here, but I leaped on Grace's sudden indifference to Shakespeare as another sign that she missed me as much as I missed her.

While Mr. Reynolds lectured about Brutus and how, at first, the guy looked up to Caesar, but then, after being swayed by Cassius, he plunged a knife into Caesar's belly, I couldn't help but look at Grace to see how she might react to this summary of the plot. Grace maintained her stony face. How was it that she didn't see the connection between Cassius and Lucifer? Cassius used Brutus to do his dirty work, the way Lucifer was using Grace.

Since her expression showed nothing, I looked for clues in her appearance. Grace's roots were beginning to show, their true honey-blond color peeking from beneath the pink. And her hair wasn't spiky like a porcupine's quills anymore. Did that mean anything? Soft strands of hair now framed her face, and I was again reminded of that day in the woods. It took all of my effort not to just reach out and touch her cheek. I stopped myself when I remembered it wasn't just my own soul at risk.

The dramatic scene of Brutus stabbing Caesar on the Senate steps was nothing compared to the fight taking place inside of me. In fact, I might as well have been thousands of miles away, further away than ancient Rome, as I thought about the night Grace and I had spent together in her room. We had been safe there, under the canopy of all those pink ruffles.

As Mr. Reynolds droned on and on, I thought about Heaven. A long time ago, I'd heard that when a person died, they got to choose what their Heaven looked like. I'd never believed it, of course. But knowing what I knew, I was sure my Heaven would be a canopied bed with pink ruffles.

It was Mr. Reynolds and his intense enthusiasm for the Bard that finally called me back to the present. "Mr. Wanderman! What do you think?"

At that point, I knew what the astronauts felt like when they landed back on earth after being up in space for so long. That sense of re-entering my everyday world was, to say the least, a bit disorienting.

At first I resisted. I wanted to stay in my pink Heaven.

But then I said, "What do I think about what?" My flippant tone didn't match my honor student status, but who cared? Why should I go out of my way and act all honorable when the rules I was forced to play by were anything but?

Two rows over, Jaimie's eyes nearly popped out of their sockets. Jimmy snickered. Again, none of it mattered. At this point, detention for a bad attitude would have been the cherry on the sundae.

Instead of getting mad, Mr. Reynolds leaned over his podium and just stared at me. Unlike the intense heat that radiated from Blake's eyes, Mr. Reynold's stare was like jumping through the spray of a fire hydrant on a hundred-degree day. Something about those eyes cast a sense of peace over me, and for the first time in a long time, the heavy weight of doing battle that I'd been carrying around with me evaporated into a sort of fine mist.

"As I was saying, Mr. Wanderman." This time when Mr. Reynolds spoke, he walked over to the window, close to where Grace was sitting at her desk. As if he wanted to get his question just right, Mr. Reynolds looked up at the cloudless, blue sky before speaking. "Do you think there is room for forgiveness in what Brutus did to Caesar? I mean, if he'd had the chance, should Caesar have forgiven his friend? But more importantly, should Brutus have forgiven himself?"

The answer to me seemed obvious. How could anyone who'd looked up to someone and then hurt them that badly be forgiven for their actions? But as soon as I opened my mouth, the peace I had been feeling took over. Even if I wanted to wrestle with myself over the answer, I found that I had no other choice but to say, "Maybe."

"So you believe that, regardless of the cruelties Brutus inflicted on his friend, that forgiveness should be an option."

"Um," I said. The thing was I had no idea if that was what I really felt.

Before Mr. Reynolds could offer anything further, the bell rang and everyone started heading for the door.

At first, I thought the day would end the way every other day for a week and a half had ended, with Grace rushing through the crowd, making it impossible to grab a moment to say a word or two even if I'd had the courage. That day was different.

After I reached down for my backpack, I looked up and Grace was standing right in front of my desk. Out in the hall there was a traffic jam of kids going to their lockers. This had caused the flow of kids getting out of our class to bottle neck. I figured Grace was in the jam, stuck without anywhere else to go. Jimmy stood two people behind her, watching our every move. Being this close to her was more painful than setting myself on fire. And God knows, I knew all about that. To avoid a plague of angry wallaroos from descending on us, I sat at my desk and played with my pen.

Grace, on the other hand, wasn't up for following the rules.

"Did you mean that?" she said.

"Mean what?" I was stunned that she was actually talking to me. This close to her, I could smell the scent of flowers pouring off her skin. Forget the wallaroos. I was about to lose it.

"Did you mean that Caesar should forgive Brutus for what he'd done to him?"

I blinked. Of all the things Grace could say to me, she wanted to discuss literature?

"I guess," I said.

"Oh," Grace said. The crowd began to move and so did Grace. It wasn't until she was gone that I realized how I'd screwed up again.

CHAPTER 22

△

I knew Grace. I knew what kind of person she was and what her heart was capable of. That's why my answer was so important to her. And, as usual, I'd messed up.

I would have bet nine lifetimes that Grace was blaming herself for taking the deal Lucifer had offered her. The poor girl was probably wracking her brains wondering what life would have been like if we had stared him down together, instead of choosing to go it alone. She wasn't the only one wondering.

Why hadn't I grabbed that little moment to let her know that, no, I didn't think Caesar needed to forgive Brutus, because Brutus only did what his heart had told him to do and that's all you can really ask of a person. The real blame should be pinned on Cassius, because if he hadn't messed with Brutus' mind and heart, no one would have gotten hurt in the first place.

I needed another chance to make things right. Unfortunately, I never got it because for the rest of the week, Grace didn't show up to school. Every day, when I got to English, I'd sit and stare at the door, waiting. But every day came and went, and still no Grace. Blake was MIA as well.

A few times I'd taken my chances and said something to Jimmy. He'd wrinkled up his nose and said, "I'd let it go if I were you, Coop." Whether this was a warning or just friendly advice I didn't know, because sometimes I suspected that, like me, Jimmy didn't always have a choice as to whose team he was playing for.

On Friday, as Mr. Reynolds lectured, all I could think of was Grace. Thoughts of her in pain or lonely were making me nuts. What was worse was the idea that she was waiting for me to come rescue her. Instead, I sat at my desk helplessly, staring at the vocabulary words that Mr. Reynolds wrote on the board.

Normal teachers usually pulled words from the books they were teaching. Not Mr. Reynolds. He had a tendency to stop mid-thought and then scribble a word down. It was like the guy had a whole other conversation going on in his head that the rest of us couldn't hear.

"Torpid," Mr. Reynolds said, writing down his newest word of the day. "Sluggishness, dullness, coma." The white chalked letters stood out against the blackness of the board. Unlike my other teachers who wrote in a kind of quick chicken scratch, Mr. Reynolds wrote in a precise kind of calligraphy.

Mr. Reynolds looked at me. He had a new pair of silver-rimmed glasses, which managed to intensify the blue of his eyes. When he looked at me, I was reminded of the old guy from the Council, the one who was always nodding off. While Mr. Reynolds was alert enough, he looked at me the same way that old guy had looked at me, like he expected me to do something.

"Yes, Mr. Wanderman?" Mr. Reynolds asked.

Without realizing it, I'd put my hand up. Oh, crap!

Jaimie looked at me curiously, as if there was hope for me after all.

Forcing my hand down, I said. "Um . . . That's okay."

For the rest of the period, I stared at the clock as it ticked away the minutes. That day when the bell rang, I was ahead

173

of the crowd. A game against Central was scheduled immediately after school. Doubting Blake would miss a game, I headed straight for the gym.

When I got there, Blake wasn't at his locker. The place was already flooded with guys whipping towels at each other, and no one mentioned the fact that our star quarterback was a no-show.

Mike went by. Though I couldn't be sure about anybody, he seemed like a decent enough kid. "What's up?" I said to him. "Where's Blake?"

Mike shrugged. "Sick, I guess. Coach is putting Kyle Lawson in to play."

While the rest of them got into uniforms, I continued to glance at the door even though I knew that there was really no point.

Despite the heavy heart I was lugging around, during the game, I was surprisingly quick on my feet. Just as I'd experienced before, my feet always knew exactly how to weave around the players on the other team. In a way, I felt like Mr. Reynolds. While my body was doing one thing, my head was busy thinking about other things. Without having to think about it, I managed five interceptions and two touchdowns.

By the time I made the second touchdown, I decided to take advantage of the moment. With the crowd on their feet, I could look up and scan the bleachers. Lots of girls waved at me and cheered. Most guys would have given their right arm for a moment like this. Not me. The one person I wanted to be there was noticeably absent.

Ryan was there, though. Front and center. He stood on the edge of the field holding his video camera, recording my every move. He'd told me he was going to do it. He'd said it would cheer Mom up to see me play. Who could argue with that? Still, it made me feel like a bug under a microscope, my wings pinned back for everyone to dissect and examine.

By the time the fourth quarter rolled around, we were way ahead of Central. Making the decision for me, my hands reached for the ball and, for the heck of it, I made my third and final touchdown. When the buzzer signaled, I ran off the field. I was grateful that, for once, my mind was able to override my body, and I was able to avoid the victory lap all the other guys were taking around the field.

Alone in the locker room, I quickly stripped out of my uniform. The cheering was so ferocious, the voices echoed off of the metal lockers. For a minute I imagined that, rather than cheering, they were all laughing at me, that every one of those people, Ryan included, belonged to Lucifer's team.

A panicky thought overtook me. What if I was playing right into what Lucifer wanted and I didn't even know it? And what if Lucy hadn't ever really cut ties with her brother, but was only pretending to be one of the good guys? Goosey Lucy certainly had her charms. Just as she'd manipulated me, she could have as easily coerced Saint Pete or even the Big Guy himself into doing stuff they didn't want to do. Just like my jersey, something stunk bad.

Desperate to keep sane, and resorting to old habits, I rammed my fist into my locker. The pain that shot through my hand and up my arm was excruciating, but excruciating in a good way. What made the pain sweet was that it was a reminder that I was still alive and still had choices.

"What the fuck?" Mike said. He was the first person in the locker room. Behind him, the rest of the team trailed in. They all glanced at the locker and then at my hand like I was crazy. Maybe I was.

"No big deal, Mike," I said, opening and closing my fist to prove to him I wasn't hurt.

One guy whose name still escaped me said, "Hey, Coop. Your brother's outside. He said when you're done, he's waiting for you."

For some reason, the anger was starting to boil up inside

of me again. Looking down at my hand, I frowned. The pain had already subsided and the skin on my knuckles wasn't even scraped up. I'd been kind of hoping for a bruise.

When I walked into the hallway, Ryan was standing by the trophy case again, this time with his back to the case, his full focus on me. "Great game, Boomer!" Ryan said when he saw me. He tapped his hand on his video camera like it was the Holy Grail or something. "I got every minute," he said, excitedly.

The feeling of anger I'd felt out on the field returned. Only this time my anger was mingled with a little bit of disgust. "You've got to stop doing this, Ryan," I said.

Ryan looked at me. "What do you mean?"

"You have to stop living through me. You have to get a life." The minute the words popped out of my mouth, I regretted them. Sort of. Maybe I could have said it better, but still the message would have been the same.

"Just because things didn't go as planned doesn't mean you should just throw in the towel," I said.

The smile that had been on Ryan's face a minute ago broke apart. His expression soured, but given some time, I was sure he'd get over it. While I knew it hurt Ryan to hear it, I also knew I had to set him straight. Living in the past and being who you were in the past, those things got old quick. You had to know when it was time to move on and become the person you were really meant to be.

The trip home was as long as it was quiet. Every now and then I glanced over at Ryan. He looked more tired than mad. That was okay. I had faith that, in time, he'd find his way again.

The only thing that interrupted the quiet was my cell phone. There was a text from Mike.

2nite. 11 p.m. Rave@seaside 4 team.

As Ryan took the straightaways a little faster, I stared at the message. Mike never texted me. Something in my gut told me this text hadn't come from Mike. In fact, I doubted it had come from this reality.

CHAPTER 23

A major clue that I wasn't the same old Cooper came when I decided to sneak out of the house that night. This time when I broke house rules the reasons weren't selfish. If anything, I was trying to protect the people I loved.

What with running back and forth to the hospital and trying to keep things as close to normal both at home and at work, Dad had run out of steam. When I passed his room on the way downstairs, I made sure to be super quiet.

As for Ryan, there was no way I was going to tell him about the rave. The guy would have burst an artery. Jocks who went to raves could potentially get busted by the police, and a police record was definitely not in Ryan's plans for me.

Getting out of the house was one thing, but getting to the rave was another problem. I thought of the Camaro. Technically, it was half mine. The only problem was that with the neighborhood tucked in for the night, the street was quiet. The Camaro's growling engine could literally wake the dead. That wasn't the only real reason I chose not to drive it. I had a bad feeling about the night, and if something happened to the Camaro, I'd feel bad on account of Ryan. He deserved that car more than I did.

Taking my chances, I decided to text Mike. He was only

a freshman and he couldn't drive legally, but I'd sensed a little hero worship going on with him, so I took my chances to see if he could get us a ride from someone. To my surprise, he texted me right back, letting me know that he'd be by to pick me up.

As I waited at the end of the driveway, I glanced back at the house. With Mom in the hospital, no one had thought to draw the curtains in the front window. Moonlight leaked in, and it was as if the house had been transported back in time. I imagined two little boys – Ryan and me – on the other side of those walls, waking up on Christmas morning, ready to plow into a mountain of presents. The memory turned to a dull ache in my chest. Neither one of us could have known how our lives would turn out.

Autumn had turned bitter, and the cold air stung my face as I continued to wait for Mike. I was careful to stand just outside of the light pouring down from the street light. If Lucifer did his work from the shadows, I needed to learn how to maneuver in the shadows, too.

I felt the thudding pulse of music before I saw the car. A few seconds later, the car's headlights pierced the darkness. My heart began to race. When I texted Mike, I'd known the risk that this, like so much else, could be a setup.

From somewhere in the distance, I heard the faint sound of a wind chime. A whooshing sound filled my ears, and my heart pounded against my chest. The adrenaline loaded into my veins gave me all the ammunition I needed to run. But did I actually think I could outrun the Devil, especially when he was driving a yellow sports car?

When the car stopped and the passenger side window rolled down, I regained some confidence.

"Where'd you get the—"

But before I could finish Mike said, "Come on."

Whether it was the same invisible force that had helped me to score all those touchdowns or my own determination, something pushed me to get in. Mike gunned the gas.

The warm, sweet-smelling air inside the car was a sharp contrast to the cold night.

"Hey! What's up, Coop!" A voice from behind me said, followed by a not-so-gentle pat on my shoulder.

Startled, I twisted around with my hands up, ready to defend myself.

"Jeez, Coop! Calm down, dude!" Mike laughed.

Because the car's back windows were tinted, I hadn't noticed the two people in the back seat. Instead of Blake or Jimmy or some other thug come to take me hostage, I recognized two other guys from the JV squad. I settled back into my seat feeling like a fool. How was I ever going to defend myself or Grace if I couldn't differentiate between these nerdy freshmen and the Prince of Darkness?

Even though the car was warm, my teeth started to chatter. Four days had passed since I'd last seen Grace. What if I was too late and Lucifer had already turned her into one of his empty, soulless minions? I thought of Grace's heart and imagined a black stain of venom in its place.

Mike palmed the steering wheel. "This is going to be great!" he said.

Looking at Mike, I noticed how bloodshot his eyes were. The redness didn't have anything to do with Lucifer, but rather the sweet smell looming in the air of the car. Mike smiled goofily. He was a good kid, but he had no idea what he was heading into. Any other time I might have set him straight, letting him know that it wasn't cool to be under anyone or anything's influence. But this wasn't the time or the place, so I just rolled down the window and breathed in some fresh air.

Mike eased the car over the bridge. At the foot of the bridge, a roadside sign lit by a large floodlight announced *Welcome to Seaside Park*. As we headed further east, a fine mist blew over us. The moon and the mist seemed to be wrestling for control. Sometimes I could make out the outline of a street sign, sometimes not. As we headed into the parking lot next to the boardwalk, the moon won out, and I could make out the outline of the Ferris wheel. The ride was closed down for the season, but its massiveness reminded me of an ogre keeping guard.

As Mike parked the car, I noticed there were no other cars in the lot. "Are you sure this is the place?"

Whether it was the weed he'd just smoked or the fact that he was just happy to have been invited to a party, Mike didn't seem to find it odd. He just shrugged and said, "This is where the text told me to park."

The four of us made our way up the ramp leading to the boardwalk, but Mike and I fell back when the other two raced ahead. The moisture from the night air made the worn wooden boards slick under my shoes, and a familiar chill slipped down my collar. Now that we were practically on top of the ocean, the fog thickened.

A few more yards and we came to the part where the arcade and a lot of the game booths and fast food joints were located. They were all boarded up tight for the season, but the smell of fried foods still lingered in the air. Another memory flashed in my head, me and Ryan shooting water into a clown's mouth with plastic water guns, racing to see who could break the balloon first.

Pop!

I spun around to see where the sound was coming from. "Relax, Coop," Mike said.

Blinking through the fog, I realized there was nothing there. Whether it was Lucifer forcing the memory on me or my own psyche fighting for survival, I resisted my fear and kept walking.

The fog was getting thicker by the minute. Mike's buddies had slipped out of sight, but from time to time I caught the heavy thud of their feet echoing up ahead. At least

I hoped they were the ones making that noise.

"Where is this place?" I whispered. Even though I couldn't see anyone, didn't mean no one was there listening. Or watching.

"Um, yeah . . . I think it's a little farther ahead," Mike said. Maybe it was just the weed wearing off, but I could tell by the little skip in Mike's voice that I wasn't the only one getting freaked out.

A voice pressed through the thickness and whispered something to me over my shoulder. "Up ahead and to the right."

At first I thought it was one of the freshmen who had doubled back to tell us he'd found the rave. But when Mike didn't react, I said, "Did you hear that?"

"Hear what?" Mike said.

"Um, nothing," I said, quickly. "I mean, I think I heard some voices down this way." Refusing to consider who it was who'd just whispered in my ear, I did what the voice told me to do.

The vibration coming from under my feet was the first clue we were heading in the right direction. The music at the rave was pounding so loud that it shook everything, not just the wooden boardwalk. The party was set up in the carousel house. Like everything else, it was boarded up tight, but someone had managed to pry a few boards open. We slipped through the opening.

The place was lit up with strobe lights and a few strands of Christmas lights carelessly looped around the poles of the carousel. There was a live band. Music pounded in my ears as dozens of bodies gyrated to the pulsing beat. People stretched their hands up in the air. It was like being thrown into a pot with a hundred drowning people, all looking to be rescued.

"You okay, Coop?" Mike said. Had it not been for Mike's wide, innocent face, I would have assumed that I'd just walked straight through the gates of Hell.

"Yeah. I'm good," I lied.

Someone reached out from the crowd, and with very little resistance on his part, Mike was pulled into the mosh pit.

"See you later, Coop!" Mike yelled back as he was quickly consumed.

Since the hand that had grabbed him wore pink nail polish, I was only slightly fearful for Mike's soul. Besides, there was only one soul I was hoping to save.

As I walked around the edge of the mosh pit, another gaggle of hands reached out. At first I resisted, but realizing it might be the only way to scan the crowd, I allowed myself to get pulled into the pit. What amazed me most about the sensation was that it felt a lot like dying. There was a certain indescribable weightlessness to the experience. The only difference was that the first time I'd died, I'd gone only because I'd felt as if I'd run out of other options. This time, I was hoping to create another option for both Grace and me.

Once in the mosh pit, I didn't need to will my body to move; the wall of writhing bodies filled in the empty pockets of my motionlessness. The strobe lights were the visual expression of the sound. In between the bursts of light and darkness, I studied all the faces around me. None of those faces belonged to Grace.

The carousel house was huge, made even bigger by the fact that the horses had been dismounted from their poles for the winter. A series of thick burlap tarps were draped over part of it to create a kind of tent. Was this where Blake was holding Grace? I pushed through a group of sweat-soaked people who were too out of their minds to notice just how sweat-soaked they were.

When I got close to the tent, I saw an outline of more writhing bodies silhouetted against the tarp. The tent looked as if it was about to explode. Instead of backing away, I took a breath and dove in.

The strobe lights couldn't penetrate the tarp, but it looked and felt just as sinister. The ornate paintings of mermaids and dolphins staring down from above me reinforced my first impression that we were drowning. Inside the tent, I found more bodies and more faces. Again, none belonged to Grace.

Clawing my way out of the tent, I was starting to think that this was all a waste of time. I imagined that somewhere Blake was sitting at a sports bar alongside Lucifer, both of them chomping on peanuts and laughing.

As I craned my neck, trying to find Mike in the sea of people, I looked up and saw the wide catwalk running along the perimeter of the building. From this angle and with the limited light, I made out the shapes of what looked like three people. Unlike the rest of the people at the rave, these bodies were relatively still, as if their amusement came from observing everyone else. A flash of light from the strobe illuminated one corner of the ceiling and my heart nearly jumped out of my mouth. Grace!

And next to Grace was Blake. I could tell from Blake's expression that he was enjoying every minute of this.

Another flash of light infiltrated Blake's nook. I craned my neck some more to catch sight of who the other person next to Blake was, but the figure remained cloaked in darkness.

Getting through the crowd was like swimming against the current. The strength of all of those people trying to keep me in the flow with them was supernaturally strong. When I finally managed to make my way to the edge of the crowd, I bumped around in the dark, searching for the set of stairs that led up to the catwalk. They were a lot easier to find than I had thought. Why hadn't I noticed them sooner?

I raced up the stairs and there they were, Blake, with Grace in front of him, his arm pulled tightly across the top of her chest. Where was the other person I had seen? Turning quickly behind me, I half expected Jimmy to come bounding out at me.

Blake laughed at me. "If it's Jimmy you're worried about, don't be. That a-hole is probably under the tent trying to get in some girl's pants!"

So if it wasn't Jimmy, then who . . . Suddenly, it hit me! Why would Lucifer want to sit in some sports bar watching me play his game when he could be watching me from box seats?

"Lucifer was here?" The words tasted so bitter in my mouth, I nearly spat them out. The idea of Heaven, Grace or any sense of hope bled out of me. A cold emptiness was all I was left with. Was this it? Had Lucifer only been playing with me before? Was this our final showdown?

"He still is. Somewhere," Blake said.

Since I'd last seen her, Grace had completed her transformation. While it was still short, Grace's hair was now back to its original honey-blond color. She'd removed all of the jewelry from her piercings, and she looked much younger, like the girl from the pictures. There was also a fear in her eyes that was terribly new.

"Grace!" I said, taking a step forward. But when I did, Blake tightened his grip so much that she coughed and her face began to lose color. He was putting pressure on her chest, literally forcing the life out of her lungs.

"Okay, okay," I said, taking a few steps back. "Just let her go, okay?"

"She's not mine to let go, Coop," Blake said. "Haven't you figured that out yet? She doesn't belong to you or me. She belongs to Him. You gave her up, remember?" But to my relief Blake released his hold a bit and some of the color returned to Grace's face.

Just like the strobe that flashed in disconnected bursts, I started to see bits and pieces of my life in still frames and suddenly realized what they all meant. Even after Lucifer had exiled me to some other life that hadn't belonged to me, deep under my skin, in a place that even the Devil couldn't send his darkness, there had always been light. That light was Grace.

"You know He's laughing at you, Coop," Blake said. "He can tell what you're thinking, and He's laughing at you."

Could Lucifer really see into my mind?

I glanced down at all those people, flailing around like a bunch of idiots. All Lucifer had to do was throw a net over them and pluck up as many as he wanted. Why did he insist on having Grace? Then it hit me. Neither Grace nor I were anything special. Lucifer was just like one of those rich guys who go on a hunt in Africa and bring back the animal they've killed so they can mount it on their wall and feel proud. Grace was just another trophy to Lucifer.

Blake moved closer to the rail, pulling Grace with him. It was hardly an effort. Compared to him, she was proportionately the weight of a stone in his hand.

"The truth is, Coop," Blake said, his voice taking on a more serious tone. "This has all been a little embarrassing to Him, what with you turning up out of the blue. I mean, the real you, that is. This whole situation has gotten a bit too messy."

Blake took a few more steps closer to the rail. My head began to spin with the realization of what he was about to do to Grace.

"It's okay, Cooper," Grace said. "I want you to be free. I shouldn't have made the choice I did. It wasn't fair to you."

"Ah, now isn't that sweet?" Blake said. His sarcasm ripped right through me, but it didn't hurt as bad as the fact that Grace was giving up.

"Please! Don't!" I said.

Blake picked Grace up and dangled her over the edge of

the rail.

Running forward, screaming, the only thing I saw was the soft tangle of honey hair hanging precariously over the rail. Blake's hands clutched her arms, but before he could make another move, I lunged.

CHAPTER 24

△

As I tumbled, the world turned black. The darkness swallowed me and the reality I had existed in a few seconds before began to bleed away at the edges.

"Grace! Grace!" I shouted. My hands grabbed at the space around me, trying desperately to find her. Had Blake thrown her over? Or had I managed to save her. But every time I reached for her, all I caught was air.

The world turned from black, to smoke, to gray, finally resting on the palest of silvers. A hard thump to my head shocked me awake. When I picked myself up, there in front of me sat the Council. It was as if I'd dreamed it all.

Lucy was the first one to remind me that, on the contrary, it had all been very, very real. "Welcome back," she said. She was as gorgeous as I remembered, only, at that moment, her beauty repulsed me so much that I wanted to strangle her.

Rushing forward, my arms ready to ring her sinewy throat, I hit something hard which rebounded me backwards.

"Invisible wall. Just a precaution, my boy," Saint Pete said.

Waving my hand out in front of me, I felt nothing.

"Where's Grace?" I yelled. "Is she . . ." I couldn't bring myself to say the word. But if she was, then why wouldn't she be here with me? Unless, just as in life, Lucifer had claimed her.

"Now, now, Cooper," Lucy said. "Give yourself a moment. I realize this has all been rather emotional for you, but there's no need to resort to old habits."

Just like before, Saint Peter sat to Lucy's right, while the other guy, whose name I still didn't know, continued to catch flies to her left. Lucy took a peanut from the old guy's dish and popped it in her mouth as if she was sitting in the movies watching a really good action flick.

Since Saint Peter seemed to be my only shot, I begged him, "Tell me where Grace is, please!"

Saint Peter cleared his throat. Then he looked down at his carefully manicured fingernails.

"Before we discuss the issue of Grace, I need to explain a few things to you, Cooper," Lucy said.

The issue of Grace! Lucy spoke as if Grace wasn't even a real person. To Lucy, Grace was only another pawn, someone she could have a bit of fun pushing around in between her manicures. What Lucy could never understand was that without Grace, Heaven and Hell didn't matter to me. Neither did she.

Even though he walked around in a shimmery robe all day, Saint Pete had also been a man a long time ago. Appealing to his ego, I said, "You're not going to let Lucy get away with this, are you?"

To my dismay, Saint Pete twitched nervously, glancing at Lucy as if waiting for her to handle this. Where was the guy's backbone?

"You didn't have any clue what she was up to! Did you?" I demanded.

Lucy smirked. The idea that my fate, as well as Grace's, was resting on Lucy's spray tanned shoulders, only fueled the flame of my rage more. This time when I lunged at the Council, I took a running start.

No luck. I landed on my ass again.

I glared at the two of them. I would have glared at all three, but the old coot at the end of the table just kept on sleeping. Every once in a while, he would make a little snuffling sound, but that was about it. Even if he could stay awake long enough, I doubted he'd be of any help.

Saint Pete finally found his tongue. "I admit that I was aware of Lucinda's highly unorthodox methods," he said.

Then, as if we were in a court room and there was a stenographer somewhere nearby, Saint Pete said, "Let it be noted for the record that I did express my concern to the administration." A fierce rumble followed Saint Pete's comment.

"The administration?" I was shocked. "You mean even God knew about this?"

"Who do you think came to me about it first?" Lucy giggled. It was obvious she was eating up every morsel of my confusion. "Even God gets tired of seeing things done the same way day in and day out. Especially when the results are less than impressive. He was tired of the methods that the present team has been employing for eons. Methods, I'd like to add, that have done little to rehabilitate humanity."

"Humanity schmanity!" Saint Peter sniffed. "All He cares about is productivity!"

Another rumble, this one much louder than the first, rippled through the room. Saint Pete's face turned the same color as his robe.

Lucy regarded me again. "Having worked alongside my brother all these years, I have been privy to – how shall I put this – certain insider secrets. God appreciated my ideas. He said he likes my creativity. And my spunk!" Lucy smiled, while Saint Pete looked ready for martyrdom.

"So, are you happy now?" I demanded. "Did your creative methods earn you the corner office with a view, Lucy?"

"It's not like that, Cooper," Lucy said.

"No? Then explain to me just what it is like!"

"Okay, but first you have to calm down. After all, if you don't, all my hard work will have been for nothing. And that would . . . depress me."

God forbid Lucy should be depressed even if it meant the rest of us were left swinging in the breeze! Calming down was the last thing on my mind. What I really wanted to do was rip out every last one of Lucy's hair extensions.

Knowing this would only get me slapped in the face by an invisible wall, I bit my tongue. Keeping my tone level, I said, "Okay. Explain."

As if she'd been preparing for this dramatic moment for some time, Lucy took a breath. "You see, Cooper, for years I've been observing the same thing. People are born, people live and they mess up. Then they come up here and they never really get a chance to redeem themselves."

Saint Pete looked annoyed. Chancing another slap on the hand from the Higher Ups, he said, "I think my bailout idea was highly successful."

Lucy rolled her eyes and ignored him. Then she continued. "One day I had this idea. If people could recycle old gum wrappers and turn them into cute little purses, why couldn't we do the same thing with people? Recycle, I mean, not turn them into purses. Lucifer thought I was out of my mind. An idealist, he called me. You see, Lucifer always preferred the tough love approach."

Lucy adjusted her robe. "My brother isn't the only one who has that attitude. Unfortunately, even people on this side of the clouds believe some humans don't have the potential to rebound from such hurts."

Saint Peter coughed, but didn't say anything.

While I didn't much appreciate being compared to a gum wrapper, I actually did see the point Lucy was making here. If I'd never found my way back to Grace, who knows what would have happened to me or my soul? Not that my current situation was one hundred percent guaranteed. For all I knew, the fate of my soul was trash, just like most gum wrappers.

Lucy sure could gab. There was even more to her story. "So, one day, I approached Him with my idea and He loved it," she said. "He was particularly interested in your story, Cooper. *And* the deal Lucifer had struck with poor Grace."

It was unbelievable. Even God wasn't beyond proving a point these days. It wasn't the afterlife. I'd landed in the middle of a Fortune 500 board meeting!

Then I realized something. Lucy hadn't just said Grace, but *poor* Grace. Was it possible this She-Devil had a shred of emotion tossing around in that cold heart of hers?

Stoking the one ember of decency I hoped existed in Lucy's heart, I said, "So, are you happy, Luce? Did you get what you wanted?"

For the first time I saw a crack in Lucy's carefully composed expression. She bit her bottom lip so hard, a tiny bubble of blood, a shade brighter than her lipstick, formed. "Well, I must admit, it has proven a bit more complicated than I anticipated."

"What do you mean?"

"While you have redeemed yourself rather nicely, I didn't think much about Grace. Since she so clearly belonged to my brother, I was willing to accept her as collateral damage. But now . . ."

Ignoring her remark about collateral damage, I grabbed onto the slim rope Lucy was tossing my way. "So there's hope?"

Lucy frowned and I could see she needed another nudge.

Appealing to Lucy's ego big time, I said, "So, if you can redeem me, just think how impressed God would be if you spited your brother and won Grace's soul back!"

I prayed that Lucy would go for my plan.

Lucy's eyes widened and she gripped the arms of her chair as if she was trying hard not to blast off. "Can we do that?" she said, checking with Saint Pete.

Before he could answer, I rushed in. "Why not?" I said, trying my hardest to maintain a casual, off-the-cuff tone. "You've already proven that you've got it going on."

"Of course! Why not?" Lucy said, triumphantly. But then a veil of doubt fell over her face. "But, logistically, how can I redeem Grace's soul when Lucifer has such a tight grip on her?"

Lucy made a sound argument, but who cared about logic. "Not as tight as the grip I have on Grace's heart," I said. "Let me go back to Earth! I want to be with Grace."

Lucy sat back in her chair, her grin telling me I still had a chance.

"This is too much, Lucy! Too, too much," Saint Pete complained. "I have sat here and idly watched as you fool with everything that is both right and sacred. If you honestly believe that I am going to let you send this boy back for the second time, so help me Lucy, I . . ."

This time it wasn't a loud crashing sound that interrupted Saint Pete's tirade, but rather a noble, if sleepy sounding voice. "Brother, I am but one humble servant. But a servant, nonetheless. I must say, I am quite taken by this young gentleman's request." The words, which sounded strangely familiar, were coming from Saint Sleepy himself.

Lucy giggled while Saint Pete stared incredulously at the man. He was awake again, and I finally got a good look at the old codger. There was something familiar about the guy. And then it hit me. For the last few weeks, I'd been staring at that same face, every day in English.

"William Shakespeare?" I was dumbfounded.

"At your service," he said. The only thing missing was the ruffled collar.

"What are you doing here?" I asked him. I imagined writers had their own place in the afterlife and that place looked something like the New York Public Library.

Shakespeare smiled. "I'm spinning stories, young gentleman. Spinning stories." He looked like he was about to drift off to sleep again.

As hard as I'd been trying to hold myself back, I couldn't help myself. "Stories? Is that all we are to you people? Just some kind of cheap entertainment?"

There was another rumble. Lucy, along with the other two clowns, eyed the sky warily. Had I finally hit a nerve?

The three of them huddled together. After a few minutes of debating, Saint Pete said, "It turns out that William has taken a real liking to you, Cooper. He has agreed to continue looking after you."

I stared at William Shakespeare. For the past few weeks, this man had been, in part, the bane of my existence. How much time had I used up in an attempt to figure out what the heck he was trying to say? Then again, Willy had provided the words Grace used to tell me that she loved me. The guy couldn't be all that bad, I reasoned.

"Wait a minute," I said, suddenly realizing something. "You said that he would *continue* looking after me?"

"Tis true," Willy said. The next thing I knew the old man was dipping his hand into the peanut bowl and throwing peanuts at me. "Catch!" he said.

I watched in wonder as the peanuts turned into silvery pebbles. The pieces clanked up against the wall, making it through my invisible cage.

Picking up one of the silver peanuts, I remembered the harpist at the restaurant, the football player who had come out of nowhere, Jaimie's braces, and Mr. Reynolds' shimmery socks.

As I pictured them, he chuckled.

"Angels," Willy said. "My own team. When I saw you

194

needed a little help, I pitched in."

Lucinda stared at him in shock.

"What?" Willy said to her. "Angels are God's breath."

"And they don't unionize," Saint Pete chimed in. Clearly, he was impressed.

This time Saint Pete was the one to send me back. With one wave of his hand, he said, "Hasta la vista!"

And I was gone.

CHAPTER 25

△

I traveled through the now familiar sequence of colors. First black, then smoke, then the softest of silvery grays.

"Cooper?"

A warm trickle of ooze dripped from my ear, and I tried lifting my hand to check it out. Oh crap! Not only did I have some serious leakage issues, but my arm was pinned to my side.

"Cooper!" This time when the voice said my name, it was noticeably female and very, very insistent.

What with the '66 Mustang parked on my chest, I found it impossible to answer.

Another voice, this one male and slightly hysterical, mirrored my opinion on the situation. "Oh, man. He's so screwed."

"Cooper! Please wake up. It's me."

Willing my eyelids to peel back, I couldn't believe it. What I'd thought was a '66 Mustang turned out to be something even more beautiful.

"Grace?"

"Oh my God! Cooper!" Grace pressed her face into mine. Her warm tears flooding into my ears cleared up any concerns I'd had about brain drain.

Lying on my back that way, I looked up and saw the

pitched roof of the carousel house. Early morning light poured through a skylight I hadn't noticed the night before, illuminating the metal walkway lining the perimeter of the building.

Shrugging off the pain in my arm, I got to my feet. "He's still up there. I have to . . ." But even without the pain in my arm, my body couldn't argue with the spinning class that was taking place in my head at the moment.

"Whoa there, buddy!" Whoever was attached to the other voice caught me and eased me back onto the floor.

Twisting my head, I watched as Mike cut up pieces of electric tape.

"You broke your arm in the fall," Grace explained.

"Yeah, good thing for you I was a Boy Scout," Mike said.

As Mike fashioned a makeshift splint using the tape and two scraps of wood he'd found, I looked at Grace. "Where's Blake?" I said, choosing my words cautiously. Mike might have been acting like a Boy Scout, but I still couldn't be one hundred percent sure.

"Blake's gone," Grace said.

"He got away?"

Grace shook her head. "No, after you went over the rail, he pulled me back."

"Why would he do that when he was so hell bent on hurting you?" I questioned.

"I don't know. I can't explain it exactly, but I saw something in his eyes. He looked less evil. Maybe watching you fall was enough to snap him out it."

My head pulsed with more questions. With my good arm, I reached out to touch Grace's cheek. "And you? You're okay?" I said, wincing in pain.

"Yeah, I'm okay. But you?" She looked up at the catwalk. Tears rimmed her eyes.

Mike put the splint in place. "Yeah, Coop. A couple of

feet over and we wouldn't be having this conversation that's for sure. Lucky for you that scaffolding was there."

"Scaffolding?" I said.

Mike pointed over his shoulder. Tucked in a corner sat one of those mechanical platforms window washers use to raise themselves in order to reach really high windows. Why hadn't I noticed it before? The really odd thing was that the contraption had been set midway between the catwalk and ground level making it the perfect height to scare the crap out of me, but not kill me.

Reading my mind, Grace said, "You were spared."

But who'd spared me? Was it Lucy wanting to show her brother who really wore the pants in the family? Or was it Lucifer wanting to keep me around a little bit longer so he could get his kicks torturing me some more?

Grace squeezed my good hand bringing me back to reality. "The important thing is that, we're *both* okay." The way she looked at me and the way she emphasized the word *both* was enough to help me relax a little.

"Jeez, Coop. Who knew a little bit of weed could make a person go nuts like that," Mike said.

Grace looked at me knowingly.

"Yeah. I guess I won't be smoking that crap anymore."

Mike put the last strip of electric tape in place. "You freaked everyone out. I never saw a place clear out so fast."

I looked at the empty cups and bits of paper littering the floor. They were the only evidence of anyone having been there.

Mike examined his handy work.

"Mike stayed here to make sure you were okay, but everyone else scattered. Cowards," Grace said bitterly.

It wasn't what Grace said but what she wasn't saying that mattered. I knew the one coward she was thinking of. Now when she talked about him, I noticed there was a lot less fear in Grace's voice. Her eyes glinted and the flush was back in her cheeks. I wasn't the only one who'd cheated death.

With Grace's help, Mike lifted me to my feet.

Outside, it really was a new day. The sun had burned off the last of the fog, and even the boarded up buildings looked less sinister.

Mike found us a bench that looked out on the ocean. "You two sit here. I'll go get the car."

With Mike gone, I could finally comfort Grace the way I wanted to. Wrapping my good arm over her shoulder, I drew her close. "You don't have to hold back anymore," I told her. "It's all going to be okay."

Grace looked at me, her eyes wide like she was seeing the world for the very first time. She took a breath in and held it for what seemed forever before she finally said, "Are you sure?"

As if the Council was giving me a reminder that there were no guarantees, a sharp pain shot through my arm. I winced. Of course I couldn't be sure. All I knew was what my heart wanted to be true.

Before I could give Grace a real answer, Mike was back. "I've got the car running. Let's go."

Grace was helping me to my feet, and Mike was just about to help when I looked down "Is that a peanut?" I asked.

I picked it up. It *was* a peanut, a silver one. I started to laugh.

"Dude, are you like still high?" Mike said.

I curled my hand over Grace's, the peanut tucked inside like a good luck charm. "Just high on life, dude." I laughed. Then I kissed Grace. Her love was all I needed to believe that we'd be okay after all.

199

ABOUT THE AUTHOR

Toni De Palma is the award winning author of *Under the Banyan Tree*, *Jeremy Owl* and *Miracle Meggie*. Toni holds an MFA from Vermont College and she is a recipient of a New Jersey Arts Council Fellowship. She also writes plays. Toni lives with her family at the Jersey shore. You can follow Toni on Facebook.

Acknowledgements

Thank you to Maer Wilson and Jen Ryan for all your dedication. You rock!

Also from Ellysian Press

Ellysian Press publishes quality speculative fiction in the following genres:

Fantasy
Science Fiction
Paranormal
Paranormal Romance
Horror
And Young Adult novels in all of the above

The following pages highlight a few of our authors.

Premonition by Agnes Jayne

Emily Von Peer hopes she never meets the man of her dreams.

For years, she's been haunted by visions of an unknown lover. But after the death of her aunt and her return to her family's estate, the dreams change. Every night she sees her imaginary lover die in her arms, until she comes face to face with him in broad daylight.

Nicholas Flynn is an Agent of Paladin, an enterprise dedicated to the study and eradication of demons. Seeking answers to a slew of magically related murders, including her aunt's, Emily joins him in the investigation.

When their exchange with a demon goes awry, Emily sustains an injury that threatens to turn her into a monster - and thrusts her into the crosshairs of sorcerers, senators, and a seductive stranger who promises eternity.

The Boogeyman by Lillie J. Roberts

The nightmare begins…
Two girls lost on a lonely country road.
One killer thrilled with an unexpected opportunity.
Two families desperate to find their lost children.
One girl…lost
One girl remains…
Until a young boy joins her…

And discovers the Boogeyman is real.

Relics by Maer Wilson

Most of Thulu and La Fi's clients are dead. Which is perfect since their detective agency caters to the supernatural. But a simple job finding a lost locket leads to a big case tracking relics for an ancient daemon.

The daemon needs the relics to keep a dangerous portal closed. His enemy, Gabriel, wants the relics to open the portal and give his people access to a new feeding ground – Earth.

Caught on live TV, other portals begin to open and the creatures of magic return to Earth. The people of Earth are not alone, but will soon wish they were.

When Gabriel threatens their family, Thulu and La Fi's search becomes personal. The couple will need powerful help in the race to find the relics before Gabriel does. But maybe that's what ghostly friends, magical allies and daemonic clients are for.

When the creatures of myth and magic return to Earth, they're nothing like your mother's fairy tales.

Exiles of Forlorn by Sean T. Poindexter

It all began when the old man died.

On a ship of exiles bound for the edge of civilization, he passes on his life's work to a band of youths. He gives each of them a piece of information that leads to a mythical treasure.

The five friends – the lord's son, the soldier, the thief, the beautiful river pirate and the wizard's apprentice – all agree to join the hunt.

They arrive on the shores of Forlorn eager to begin their journey, but find a community plagued by threats from pirates and man-eating giants. The friends must choose to either stay and help those who have taken them in or to venture into unknown lands in search of a prize that may not even exist.

Either choice promises excitement, danger — and death.

ELLYSIAN PRESS

To find other Ellysian Press books, please visit our website (http://www.ellysianpress.com/).

Some of our thrilling novels include:

Premonition by Agnes Jayne

Moth by Sean T. Poindexter

The Boogeyman by Lillie J. Roberts

Exiles of Forlorn by Sean T. Poindexter

Relics by Maer Wilson

A Shadow of Time by Louann Carroll

Idyllic Avenue by Chad Ganske

Portals by Maer Wilson

Innocent Blood by Louann Carroll

Magics by Maer Wilson

The Ellysian Press Catalog has a complete list of current and forthcoming books.